P...

WHO IS MARK TWAIN?

"What's most remarkable about this collection of Twain's work is that, more than 100 years after he wrote these stories, they remain not only remarkably funny but remarkably modern. . . . Ninety-nine years after his death, Twain still manages to get the last laugh." —*Vanity Fair*

"As funny and insightful as any of his published and well-known works, these essays take on the federal government, religion, race, fame, and even the literary canon with a sharp-eyed clarity we can chuckle over as we read while feeling uncomfortable knowing that they feel all too contemporary." —The Daily Beast

"Most of all, though, *Who Is Mark Twain?* is worth reading for the sheer pleasure of rediscovering why this writer was so popular in his day." —*Los Angeles Times*

"Twain once famously wrote: 'The reports of my death are greatly exaggerated.' This book proves that he continues to enjoy literary immortality." —*South Florida Sun-Sentinel*

WHO IS
MARK TWAIN?

ALSO BY MARK TWAIN

The Innocents Abroad

Roughing It

The Gilded Age

The Adventures of Tom Sawyer

A Tramp Abroad

The Prince and the Pauper

Life on the Mississippi

Adventures of Huckleberry Finn

A Connecticut Yankee in King Arthur's Court

The Tragedy of Pudd'nhead Wilson

Personal Recollections of Joan of Arc

Following the Equator

{ WHO IS
MARK TWAIN? }

by **MARK TWAIN**

harperstudio

An Imprint of HarperCollins*Publishers*

Designed by Leah Carlson-Stanisic

Library of Congress Cataloging-in-Publication Data

Twain, Mark, 1835–1910.
    Who is Mark Twain? / by Mark Twain. — 1st ed.
       p. cm.
    ISBN 978-0-06-173501-1 (pbk.)
    1. Twain, Mark, 1835–1910. 2. Authors, American—19th century—Biography. I. Title.

    PS1331.A2 2010b
    818'.409—dc22
    [B]
                                                                    2010001430

10 11 12 13 14   OV/RRD   10 9 8 7 6 5 4 3 2 1

CONTENTS

CONTENTS

"STACKS OF LITERARY REMAINS"
A NOTE ON THE TEXT

Y ou had better shove this in the stove," Mark Twain said at the top of an 1865 letter to his brother, "for I don't want any absurd 'literary remains' & 'unpublished letters of Mark Twain' published after I am planted."

Considering that Mark Twain issued that gentle command weeks before he had published his first big success, "Jim Smiley and His Jumping Frog," and almost two years before he published his first book, it was a remarkably prescient thing to say, even as a joke. The letter to his brother survives because his brother ignored the instruction to burn it, and Mark Twain himself soon changed his mind about what should be done with his "literary remains." Thirty-six years later, in September 1901, he told his good friend Joe Twichell that he had "done a grist of writing here this summer, but not for publication soon—if ever. I did write two satisfactory articles for early print, but I burnt one of them & have buried the other one in my large box of Posthumous Stuff. I've got stacks of Literary Remains piled up there."

This time he was clearly not joking—or exaggerating. When Mark Twain died in 1910, he left behind him the largest cache of personal papers created by any nineteenth-century American author—letters, notebooks, a massive autobiography, hundreds of unpublished literary manuscripts, seventy thousand incoming letters, photographs, bills, checks, contracts, and other business documents (easily half a million pages). All but two of the short works published here come from that archive, known as the Mark Twain Papers in The Bancroft Library at Berkeley. The other two ("The Devil's Gate" and "I Rise to a Question of Privilege") are among the earliest written, and come from a much smaller group of his manuscripts originally kept for him by his sister Pamela. That group includes two dozen unpublished sketches and essays written as early as age twenty, all of which eventually found their way to the Vassar College Library. These two archives alone show that Mark Twain's penchant for preserving manuscripts he did not publish or sometimes even finish was lifelong.

In referring to these manuscripts as "stacks of Literary Remains" Clemens would seem to imply that he expected some of them to be published, or at least read, after his death ("not for publication soon—if ever"). But how did he really feel about posterity publishing things from his "large box of Posthumous Stuff"? Aren't we trampling on his own best judgment in publishing what he himself decided not to publish? I don't think so. Let me explain why.

When the first half of the manuscript for *Huckleberry Finn* was discovered in 1991 (Mark Twain had given it to a library, but it had been lost for more than 100 years) it made quite a commotion in the press and even in the world at large. Senator Daniel Patrick Moynihan, for example, is known to have stopped his limousine in front of Sotheby's just to see the long-lost manuscript then on display there. The general feeling was, I suppose, that here at last was *the* authentic text of Mark Twain's masterpiece. About this same time, a famous New York publisher called me in Berkeley because, he said, he wanted to know just exactly what the manuscript represented: Was it really the ultimate text for *Huck Finn*? I explained that, no, it was actually not Mark Twain's *final draft*, but rather more like a *first draft*, since he had had his manuscript typed, and then extensively revised that typescript, which in turn became his final draft and went to the typesetter. The New York publisher said: "How strange. All of *my* authors go to great lengths to destroy their early drafts"—presumably so that no one can tell how they struggled to arrive at the final text.

I think it is clear that, unlike most writers, Mark Twain was not embarrassed by his "literary remains" even when they were failures. He seems to have been wholly willing to let posterity read them, unafraid of the light they might cast on his talent, or the way he wrote. That unusual willingness to let the world see how he worked, including how he failed or simply misfired, had only one precondition—*he must not be alive at the time.* The following passage from Mark Twain's autobiography (31 May 1906), whose full publication he deliberately forbade until 100 years after his death, makes this precondition explicit, and explains why he thought he was taking no real risk in the matter:

> *I can speak more frankly from the grave than most historians would be able to do, for the reason that whereas they would not be able to <u>feel</u> dead, howsoever hard they might try, I myself am able to do that. They would be making believe to be dead. With me, it is not make-believe. They would all the time be feeling, in a tolerably definite way, that that thing in the grave which represents them is a conscious entity; conscious of what it was*

*saying about people; an entity capable of feeling shame;
an entity capable of shrinking from full and frank expression, for they believe in immortality. They believe
that death is only a sleep, followed by an immediate
waking, and that their spirits are conscious of what is
going on here below and take a deep and continuous interest in the joys and sorrows of the survivors whom they
love and don't.*

*But I have long ago lost my belief in immortality—
also my interest in it. I can say, now, what I could not
say while alive—things which it would shock people to
hear; things which I could not say when alive because I
should be aware of that shock and would certainly spare
myself the personal pain of inflicting it.*

In other words, Mark Twain was perfectly willing to let us
read his most intimate manuscripts precisely because he *knew*
that when we did so, he would no longer exist.

Yet whatever intentions Mark Twain had for his manuscripts, as long as his official biographer, Albert Bigelow
Paine, had charge of them—from 1910 to 1937—he and the
author's only surviving daughter, Clara, had sole access to
them and absolute discretion over their publication. Paine, in
fact, thought most of the literary manuscripts ought not to

be published at all, although he eventually did publish small, heavily edited selections of letters, notebooks, the autobiography, a bastardized form of "The Mysterious Stranger," and two or three dozen manuscript sketches. Of course Paine implied that he was carrying out the author's intentions: "Mark Twain himself had quite definite ideas as to the disposition of his literary effects, and he left instructions accordingly—instructions that thus far [i.e., 1935] have been carried out." But no one except Paine has ever seen even a copy of those instructions, and there are good reasons to doubt that Mark Twain took so protective a view of what he had consistently saved from destruction.

Paine's successor as editor of the Mark Twain Papers, Bernard DeVoto, published several dozen more manuscripts, and prepared for publication what he thought were the best of the lot: the unfinished "Letters from the Earth" and other late stories, which were not, however, published by Harper & Row until 1962, seven years after his own death, because of Clara's objections. DeVoto was quite clear that he would publish only the very best of what he found in the papers, lest the inferior material cloud Mark Twain's reputation: "the publication of variant readings and wholly unimportant fragments should be forbidden" he wrote in 1938.

Then, in 1962, the University of California contracted with

the Mark Twain estate for the rights to publish selections from the Mark Twain Papers, which Clara had given to the University in 1949. The remaining manuscripts then began to be more or less systematically issued in a scholarly edition. Even so, after more than forty years of scholarly publishing during which a dozen or more editors have sifted through the archive and published what they thought was of interest, dozens of manuscripts, both finished and unfinished, remain. The twenty-four collected here represent an across-the-board sampling from different genres and different time periods, weighted slightly toward pieces that can stand more or less on their own, without much explanation.

It is important to say that these works are not being offered here as a group of overlooked masterpieces that will somehow begin to compete with Mark Twain's most famous work. In large part, their interest lies elsewhere—in what they show us about how Mark Twain worked as a writer. But it would also be a mistake to assume that they were left unpublished because he thought they fell short of his usual standard. Any random sampling will turn up the usual signs of his genius, the typical precision and sparkle of his prose, always capable of surprising us into smiling at some shameful trait of the damned human race. They are so well crafted, clear, and wickedly funny (even when he left them incomplete) that their non-publication must be explained by particular circumstances, not his judgment that they were inferior work and therefore not worth publishing.

Seven of the manuscripts are unfinished, breaking off abruptly—left sometimes without a title, let alone a conclusion. They are vivid testimony to Mark Twain's restless and often quite daring inventiveness, his lifelong habit of seizing upon an idea for an article or story and simply plunging into the telling of it, with hardly a clue as to where he might end up. In "Whenever I Am about to Publish a Book" the text comes to a halt just as he promises to reproduce unaltered quotations from reviews of his "last book" (probably *The Prince and the Pauper*). Did he suddenly think better of giving such attention to foolish comments on his work? Or was he just distracted by something, and still hoping for a chance to complete the essay? We simply don't know.

"Frank Fuller and My First New York Lecture," which is really a draft of a lecture Mark Twain planned to use on his around-the-world-tour of 1895–96, comes to an end (not coincidentally, I think) when the bitterly remembered reason for the lecture tour—his need to pay off the debts of his bankrupt publishing house—bubbles to the surface. He never gave this lecture, the very conception of which seems palpably modern in several ways—a hilarious send-up of our foolish preoccupation with celebrity, built around the story of his own search for fame. Its modernity seems especially obvious if one takes into account its multimedia plan: he imagines projecting slides of the famous people he refers to throughout, thereby producing an illustrated lecture that begins with a more or less factual account of the run-up to his own first (highly successful) appearance on the platform in New York, in May 1867.

Although I was utterly unknown, every one of the most celebrated men of that day, was invited to come. It has always been my pride that that distinction was shown me. I hope it will not be regarded as immodest in me if I name some of these. First in the list by every right is Grant—scene-photograph—anecdote (grand description of his services.) General Grant—he was not able to come. Sheridan—scene-photograph—had just finished his great Indian campaign, and was tired—of disturbances—and—he was not present.

Sherman—scene-photo—Lt. Gen—was head of the Army and was reforming the rest of it—he did not need reforming himself—and was obliged to be absent.

Gen. Thomas—he couldn't come.

Gen. Logan wanted to come, but was not well and could not sleep where there was noise.

Admiral Farragut—just at that time a child was born to—not to <u>him</u>, and I don't remember now who it was born to, and now I come to think, I believe it was not born that year—but anyway he couldn't come.

And so on, until we get the joke, and want only to see what other excuses he can come up with. Yet even after writing more than fifty pages of manuscript, he set it aside and replaced it with something entirely different. Indeed, the piece is so much an unfinished draft that it begins with what are in effect notes to himself. These shade without a break into the narrative proper, showing us quite graphically how he often *felt* his way into a new work.

"Conversations with Satan" begins, I think, brilliantly enough with Mark Twain's description of "a slender and shapely gentleman" dressed, he says, like an Anglican Bishop, who turns out to be Satan himself. The author proceeds with a "modern" interview of the Devil, beginning with small talk about the excellence of the German stove, used for heating the house or apartment:

"You use it in America, of course?"
I was pleasantly surprised at that, and said—

"Is it possible that Ihre Majestät is not familiar with America?"

"Well—no. I have not been there lately. I am not needed there."

This sort of thing is promising enough, but Mark Twain soon gets sidetracked into a long disquisition about cigars, and simply stops writing when he senses that the narrative has made too long a detour ever to get back to the main road. Typically, Mark Twain *did not throw away or destroy* even work like this, which he left unfinished, and often seemed unable to finish.

Most of these pieces were, however, finished—two or three articles for magazines or newspapers ("The Force of 'Suggestion'" written for *Harper's Weekly,* "Professor Mahaffy on Equality" and "On Postage Rates on Authors' Manuscript" for unspecified journals); snatches of pure autobiography ("A Group of Servants," "An Incident," "Dr. Van Dyke as a Man and a Fisherman," and "Happy Memories of the Dental Chair"); letters to the editor ("The Missionary in World-Politics" and "I Rise to a Question of Privilege"); a literary burlesque ("The Undertaker's Tale"); two original fables ("The Quarrel in the Strong-Box" and "The Jungle Discusses Man"); a short story

("Telegraph Dog"); literary criticism ("Jane Austen"); and even several travel-book chapters (or passages) that he wrote for but ultimately excluded from *A Tramp Abroad* ("The Music Box" and "The Grand Prix") and *The Innocents Abroad* ("The Devil's Gate"). They were all written between 1868, when Clemens was thirty-three, and 1905, when he was seventy. So why didn't he publish them? The reasons are almost as numerous as the pieces themselves.

In some cases they were experiments, practice for more ambitious or more successful work, or just something to test against one of his usual pre-publication readers. We know that Bret Harte, for instance, at Mark Twain's request, read the entire manuscript for *The Innocents Abroad* and recommended several cuts, including "The Devil's Gate," originally part of chapter 21, where Mark Twain describes Italian scenery. Harte commented in the margin *"apropos des bottes"* (that is, apropos of nothing) and Mark Twain took it out. He tried again, in 1882, to weave this anecdote into *Life on the Mississippi*, and was again advised to take it out, which he did. That later version has been published, but "The Devil's Gate" has not.

"The Undertaker's Tale" stands out here as something Mark Twain had tested (unfavorably) against his own personal "focus group." He seems to have been slow to grasp exactly why it failed, or even to agree that it did fail. The basic idea, also quite modern (think "Six Feet Under"), was to throw a typical Horatio Alger hero into a family of undertakers (ladies and gentlemen, meet the Cadaver family) and then let the formulaic story work itself out. Paine reminds us that during the summer months Mark Twain typically spent the day writing, up on a hill above the family home in Elmira, at the end of which he descended and read aloud his day's work to the family:

> Once, when for a day he put aside other matters to record a young undertaker's love-affair, and brought down the result in the evening, fairly bubbling with the joy of it, he met with a surprise. The tale was a ghastly burlesque, its humor of the most disheartening, unsavory sort. No one spoke during the reading, nobody laughed. The air was thick with disapproval. His voice lagged and faltered toward the end. When he finished there was heavy silence. Mrs. Clemens was the only one who could speak. "Youth, let's walk a little," she said.

A few weeks later Mark Twain asked his friend William Dean Howells to "tell me what is the trouble with it." We don't know what Howells told him, but Mark Twain obviously did not throw the manuscript away. It is published in full for the first time here, and very possibly for the first audience capable of appreciating its humor as the author intended.

"Happy Memories of the Dental Chair" is manifestly autobiographical, and possibly incomplete—a report of his first encounter with a dentist, but in this case a rather extraordinary one: John Mankey Riggs of Hartford, who gave his name to Riggs's Disease (what your dentist would call "pyorrhea"). Mark Twain is here characteristically fascinated by technical procedures, including Riggs's part in the discovery and use of anesthetic: "an event of such vast influence, magnitude, importance, that one may truly say it hardly has its equal in human history." Much as he admires Riggs for his part in that discovery, he also has him squarely in his sights: "He was gray and venerable, and humane of aspect; but he had the calm, possessed, surgical look of a man who could endure pain in another person." Riggs died in 1885, shortly after this sketch was written, and that may have been partly why Mark Twain did not publish it.

Mark Twain also declined to publish, or sought to publish anonymously, things he thought would so outrage his audience that he would lose their support and undermine his family's income. These are not heavily represented in this selection, but "The Missionary in World-Politics" manifestly qualifies. Its barely suppressed rage at European exploitation of the

Chinese was intended for publication in the London *Times* shortly after the Siege of Peking, during the Boxer Rebellion. On 16 July 1900, Clemens wrote a cover letter for the manuscript to C. Moberly Bell, one of the *Times*'s editors, but he never sent either. The piece itself is not signed "Mark Twain," but rather "X"—such sharply critical things could only be published, if at all, behind a cloak of anonymity. "Don't give me away, whether you print it or not" he wrote Bell. It seems likely that he decided not to send it when the news reached him that the "massacre of the Ministers" (referred to bitterly in the penultimate paragraph) was only a false rumor, most of the diplomats having survived being attacked by the Boxers. In any case, Mark Twain's withering denunciation of cultural imperialism—the cynical use of the missionaries by "the Concert of Christian Birds of Prey" to exploit the Chinese—has lost none of its relevance for today. "My sympathies are with the Chinese," he wrote privately to Twichell. "They have been villainously dealt with by the sceptered thieves of Europe, & I hope they will drive all the foreigners out & keep them out for good. I only wish it; of course I don't really expect it." (He was less than a year away from his decision to publicly criticize American imperialism in the Philippines, beginning with a justly famous essay titled "To the Person Sitting in Darkness.")

This pattern of second thoughts arising to restrain publication is evident throughout his career. "I Rise to a Question of Privilege" was written in May 1868 in direct response to a public rebuke he received from a Baptist clergyman in San Francisco—"and in very good grammar, too, for a minister of the gospel." It was prepared specifically for publication in the San Francisco *News Letter and California Advertiser,* but Mark Twain probably never sent it, having thought twice about the effect so frank a critique of conventional religion might have on his then still fragile reputation. And he did not even finish writing "Interviewing the Interviewer," an 1870 sketch written to retaliate against criticism aimed at him by Charles A. Dana, the famous editor of the New York *Sun,* almost certainly because he realized the futility of such public combat.

Eventually, in the last decade of his life, Mark Twain evolved the habit of writing what he wanted to write, no matter how incendiary, knowing all the while that he would not publish it, but simply put it into that "box of Posthumous Stuff" and let it be published after his death. He stipulates to this strategy in "The Privilege of the Grave," written on 18 September 1905, the thesis of which is that a dead man "has one privilege which is not exercised by any living person: free speech." Most of us, most of the time, suppress the truth about our genuine beliefs. "Sometimes we suppress an opinion for reasons that are a credit to us, not a discredit, but oftenest we suppress an unpopular opinion because we cannot afford the bitter cost of putting it forth. None of us likes to be hated, none of us likes to be shunned." Of the pieces published here, perhaps only the dialect sketch called "The Snow-Shovelers" falls into this category. Its devilish needling of the "socialis" and the "anerkis" is quietly conveyed through the earnest conversation of two black laborers "in the elegant-residence end of a large New England town." (Mark Twain lived in Hartford at the time, and doubtless overheard the real-life exchange that he here turned into satirical fiction.) But the finished piece was probably made to seem inappropriate by the Haymarket Riot of 4 May 1886, in which ostensible "anarchists" killed more than a dozen policemen and civilians with a bomb, and it remained unpublished.

Taken together, these short works give us a window into Mark Twain's literary workshop, a fresh glimpse of his remarkable talent, lavished even on work he decided, for various reasons, not to publish. Most of them are quite capable of standing on their own merits: shrewdly observed, written with preternatural clarity, and often very funny, they are not simple rejects. Their range of subjects and techniques is itself impressive, even when Mark Twain declined to complete his own experiment. And for these and other reasons, I hope their publication now will pique the curiosity of today's readers about just who Mark Twain is. The success of his masterpiece, *Huckleberry Finn,* has tended to overshadow the fact that he experimented constantly in various short forms, even in the things he *published* during his long career. Public curiosity about him and what he wrote in this vein goes back to at least November 1865, when his friend Charles Henry Webb said that to his way of thinking, "Shakspeare had no more idea that he was writing for posterity than Mark Twain has at the present time, and it sometimes amuses me to think how future Mark Twain scholars will puzzle over that gentleman's present hieroglyphics and occasionally eccentric expressions." Not even Webb, however, anticipated that "future Mark Twain scholars" and readers would still be encountering previously unpublished work of this quality, a century after his death in 1910.

ROBERT H. HIRST
General Editor, Mark Twain Project

Note: I have described all twenty-six pieces as "previously unpublished," by which I mean not printed or otherwise made readily accessible to the general reader. More strictly speaking, all of them were included in a microfilm edition issued by the Mark Twain Project in 2001. Also in 2001 twenty-two of these twenty-six pieces were printed in *Twenty-Two Easy Pieces by Mark Twain*, a special limited edition published by the University of California Press. Four have been previously printed for a very limited audience. "Interviewing the Interviewer" and "The American Press" were included in *Mark Twain: Press Critic*, commentary by Thomas A. Leonard, published by The Friends of The Bancroft Library in 2003. "Jane Austen," with editorial comment inserted between almost every sentence, was published by Emily Auerbach in the *Virginia Quarterly Review* for Winter 1999. "The Walt Whitman Controversy" was published by Ed Folsom and Jerry Loving in the *Virginia Quarterly Review* for Spring 2007. "Happy Memories of the Dental Chair" was not printed in full but only quoted by Sheldon Baumrind in "Mark Twain Visits the Dentist," *The Journal of the California Dental Association*, in December 1964. But *Who Is Mark Twain?* represents the first time any of these manuscripts has been published for a general audience.

The date of composition if known, or an approximate range for it, is given for each manuscript. When the title is enclosed in square brackets, I have supplied it because Mark Twain left the manuscript untitled.

[Whenever I Am about to Publish a Book] *1881–1885*
[Frank Fuller and My First New York Lecture] *May–July 1895*

WHENEVER I AM ABOUT
TO PUBLISH A BOOK

Whenever I am about to publish a book, I feel an impatient desire to know what kind of a book it is. Of course I can find this out only by waiting until the critics shall have printed their reviews. I *do* know, beforehand, what the verdict of the general public will be, because I have a sure and simple method of ascertaining that. Which is this—if you care to know. I always read the manuscript to a private group of friends, composed as follows:

1. Man and woman with no sense of humor.

2. Man and woman with medium sense of humor.

3. Man and woman with prodigious sense of humor.

4.   An intensely practical person.

5.   A sentimental person.

6.   Person who must have a moral in, and a purpose.

7.   Hypercritical person—natural flaw-picker and fault-finder.

8.   Enthusiast—person who enjoys anything and everything, almost.

9.   Person who watches the others, and applauds or condemns with the majority.

10.   Half a dozen bright young girls and boys, unclassified.

11.   Person who relishes slang and familiar flippancy.

12.   Person who detests them.

13.   Person of evenly-balanced judicial mind.

14.   Man who always goes to sleep.

These people accurately represent the general public. Their verdict is the sure forecast of the verdict of the general public. There is not a person among them whose opinion is not valuable to me; but the man whom I most depend upon—the man whom I watch with the deepest solicitude—the man who does most toward deciding me as to whether I shall publish the book or burn it, is the man who always goes to sleep. If he drops off within fifteen minutes, I burn the book; if he keeps awake three-quarters of an hour, I publish—and I publish with the greatest confidence, too. For the intent of my works is to entertain; and by making this man comfortable on a sofa and timing him, I can tell within a shade or two what degree of success I am going to achieve. His verdict has burned several books for me—five, to be accurate.

Yes, as I said before, I always know beforehand what the general public's verdict will be; but I never know what the professional reviewer's will be until I hear from him. I seem to be making a distinction here; I seem to be separating the professional reviewer from the human family; I seem to be intimating that he is not a part of the public, but a class by himself. But that is not my idea. He *is* a part of the public; he represents a part of the public, and legitimately represents it; but it is the smallest part of it, the thinnest layer—the top part, the select and critical few. The crust of the pie, so to speak. Or, to change the figure, he is Brillat-Savarin, he is Delmonico, at a banquet. The five hundred guests *think* they know it is a good banquet or a bad one, but they don't absolutely *know,* until Delmonico puts in his expert-evidence. Then they know. That is, they know until Brillat-Savarin rises and knocks Delmonico's verdict in the head. After that, they don't know what they do know, as a general thing.

Now in my little private jury I haven't any representative

of the top crust, the select few, the critical minority of the world; consequently, although I am able to know beforehand whether the general public will think my book a good one or a bad one, I never can know whether it really *is* a good one or a bad one until the professional reviewers, the experts, shall have spoken.

So, as I have said, I always wait, with anxiety, for their report. Concerning my last book the experts have now delivered their verdict. You will naturally suppose that it has set me at rest. No, you are in error. I am as much bothered as I was before. This surprises you?—and you think my mind is wandering? Wait, and read the evidence, and you will see, yourself, that it is of an unsettling nature. I am going to be fair: I will make no quotation that is not genuine; I will not alter or amend the text in any way.

FRANK FULLER AND MY
FIRST NEW YORK LECTURE

Celebrities of the time who couldn't come (explain why) and who could. (Boss Tweed. He was there.)

Although I was utterly unknown, every one of the most celebrated men of that day, was invited to come. It has always been my pride that that distinction was shown me. I hope it will not be regarded as immodest in me if I name some of these. First in the list by every right is Grant—scene-photograph—anecdote (grand description of his services). General Grant—he was not able to come. Sheridan—scene-photograph—had just finished his great Indian campaign, and was tired—of disturbances—and—he was not present.

Sherman—scene-photo—Lt. Gen—was head of the Army and was reforming the rest of it—he did not need reforming himself—and was obliged to be absent.

Gen. Thomas—he couldn't come.

Gen. Logan wanted to come, but was not well and could not sleep where there was noise.

Admiral Farragut—just at that time a child was born to—not to *him*, and I don't remember now who it was born to, and now I come to think, I believe it was not born that year—but anyway he couldn't come.

General Lee was delayed—so was Longstreet

Commodore Vanderbilt engagement

Peter Cooper, Depew (*very* young) engagement

Horace Greeley

P. of Wales (26 or 27) photo. tried to send regrets but was overcome by his feelings.

Gladstone and Disraeli

The present Kaiser (about 3 yrs old) sent regrets—was overworked and frail in health—trying to learn German.

Longfellow, Holmes, Whittier, Bryant, Emerson, Lowell

Cleveland, mayor of Buffalo.

Andrew Johnson

•   •   •

Every one of these illustrious men was sorry, and sent regrets;—even——lamentations. But it is *something* that they *wanted* to come.

Boss Tweed, Heenan,—and have a number of photos from Sing Sing,—or a group—in penitentiary costume. These came. I do not know their names, but they were all public men and served the State.

My photo—Fuller's—both young.

F's conscience—take a shovel and dig for it.

As soon as a man recognizes that he has drifted into age, he gets reminiscent. He wants to talk and talk; and not about the present or the future, but about his old times. For there is where the pathos of his life lies—and the charm of it. The pathos of it is there because it was opulent with treasures that are gone, and the charm of it is in casting them up from the musty ledgers and remembering how rich and gracious they were.

Yes, and when a man gets old he wants to *explain* his past. He calls it that; but as a rule what he really wants to do is to whitewash it. I don't want to whitewash mine, for it doesn't need it. I have kept it in that kind of repair all the time. But I do want to explain one circumstance which has been a burden to me for 30 years; and that is, how I came to intrude upon this city—a city which had never done me any harm—and invite it to come 3,000 strong and hear me lecture in Cooper

Institute, when nobody knew who I was, or had ever heard of me. It must have seemed a strange impertinence, and indeed it was.

But it was not my fault. I was entirely without blame in the matter, and have always felt that in fairness I ought to be allowed to clear myself. I do not mean as a matter of right, but as a favor, an indulgence, a privilege. None but the old can ask a grace like this without indelicacy, and so long as I was young I bore my pain as I might, and waited for the compassions due to age to privilege me to speak.

No, it was not my fault. It was the fault of an old and particular friend of mine—a man who is still my old and particular friend—a friend who, for brevity's sake—concealment's sake—I will call Fuller—Frank Fuller. It was a great mistake that he committed—that he innocently committed. There are two private versions of the matter—his and mine. One of them is not true. I have always had more confidence in mine, because although he was older than I, he had not had as much practice in telling the truth.

He always *means* to speak the truth—no one who knows him will deny him that credit—he always *means* to speak the truth—and then forgets. He was—and is—an excellent man: fine, generous, cordial, unselfish, a man of fine and original mind, of lovable nature, of blemishless character, a sterling and steadfast friend through all weathers, a man of gracious dreams, of radiant visions, of splendid enthusiasms, colossal enthusiasms, an optimist in the zenith of whose soul the sun always shines, a magnified and ennobled Col. Sellers, a charming man—indeed, a perfect man—with that one defect. Just that one defect: that he can imitate the truth so that the Recording Angel himself would set it down in his book—and just as like as not reject statements of mine. Edit them, anyway. It is a wonderful and beautiful gift. I wish I had it. I have often tried to imitate the truth—oh, not latterly, but when I was younger—but it was not for me. It is a gift—it cannot be acquired.

I first knew Judge Fuller in Great Salt Lake City, in the summer of '61. He has always had titles. He was Archbishop Fuller then. He was not connected with any Church. It was only a decoration. It was an office which did not exist. There was no Church there but the Mormon Church, and it had only Bishops, and the Bishoprics were all full. So Fuller took the title of Archbishop because he wanted to be something, and there was no other vacancy. And he was entitled to some such reward, on account of religious services which he had rendered the Church in keeping a broker's office where wives and children and such things could be exchanged for the necessaries of life.

Next I knew him in Nevada Territory. He was ex-Governor

then; not ex-Governor of any particular commonwealth, but just ex-Governor at large. He wanted to be something, and there was no other vacancy. He was always bright, energetic, sanguine, useful. There, the public finances being low, he tried to get legalized prize-fighting introduced to save the treasury's life, but it failed—the people were not advanced enough yet.

Next, I knew him in San Francisco. He was General then. It was a brevet. He was learning the military business, and getting ready.

Later, in Arizona, he was Admiral; then he came on to New York and became Judge—and waited for a vacancy. That was nearly 30 years ago. I came on, myself, the next year. It was then that this thing happened, which I spoke of a while ago. He wanted me to lecture. I was afraid of it. I said I was not known. He said that that was merely my modesty; that I was *too* modest; much too modest; abnormally modest; morbidly modest, indecently modest. He said it was a disease and must not be allowed to run on or it would get worse. He said that so far from being unknown, I was the best known man in America except Gen. Grant, and the most popular. He went on talking like that until he made me believe that New York was in distress to hear me. He even frightened me; for he made me believe that if I stood out and refused to lecture, there would be riots. He was at white heat with one of his splendid enthusiasms, and so I was carried away by it and believed it all. For I was only a young thing—callow, trustful, ignorant of the world—hardly 33 years old, and easily persuaded to my hurt by any person with plausible ways and an eloquent tongue—and he had these.

So at last I consented, but begged him to get a small hall—a hall which would not seat more than 500—so as to cover accidents; and then if it should be overpacked we could take a large hall next time. But he would not hear of it. He said it was diffident foolishness—insanity. He said he was not acting upon guesswork, he knew what he was about. He knew it was going to be the most colossal success that New York had seen since Jenny Lind—and it was going to beat Jenny Lind, too. He was so sure of it that he was going to foot all the bills himself and if it didn't turn out as he said it wouldn't cost *my* pocket anything.

The more he talked about it the more enthusiastic he got and the more uncontrollable. First, he went off and hired the large hall of Cooper Institute; and came back distressed and mourning, because it would seat only 3,000. Why of course I was aghast. I said it was rank lunacy—that *we* couldn't have the least use for such a gigantic place like that; the audience would get lost in it, and we'd have to offer a reward. I implored him, I supplicated him to get rid of Cooper Institute; and if he couldn't, I offered to go and burn it down.

It had no effect—none in the world; he didn't even listen to me—only walked the floor and said what a pity it was that we got to talk in a little coop like that. Then he brightened up and said he knew how to fix it now—he would go and hire it for 3 weeks. I couldn't get my voice for terror—and he just marched the floor in a rapture of happiness—and finally flung out of the place, jamming his hat on his head as he went, and said he would go and hire it for 3 months. There's a time to die. *My* time. Missed fire.

So I sat down and cried. I was a young thing, and all this dreadful peril was so new to me. But he came back raging, and said the hall was engaged for months ahead, and only his one night was vacant; and moreover those people showed no proper pride or exultation in what we were going to do for them. And he had told them to their faces that we wouldn't ever lecture in their shop again.

I asked him what our date was, and he said ten days hence. Ten days! Only 10 days to advertise in? Couldn't pull a house together for Adam in 10 days. Oh, dear, I said, we haven't a show in the world. I begged him to get to work straight off with his advertising; and I offered to sit up all night and every night and help. He looked astonished; and said there was a much more serious thing than that to be looked after and thought about, and that was, what to do with 30,000 people in a house that would seat only a tenth of it.

But he said he would advertise, and he did. He spent his money as freely as if it had been somebody else's, and maybe it was—I dono where he got it. And he worked, too—worked like a steam engine. It was inspiring to see him at it. He performed prodigies. Well, you can't be in the company of forces like that and remain dead. His splendid confidence, his volcanic enthusiasm carried me out of myself again. I got to believing, once more.

The plans that that man made! He was going to have all the horse-cars in the city put on the line that ran by the hall;—bridge of cars from one end of New York to the other—couldn't *move*. He said *that* didn't make any difference, people just pay their fare and walk through and go *in*. He was going to have the neighboring streets walled by policemen to preserve order in the multitudes; he was going to have ambulances all along, to carry away people wounded in the crush—and some hearses, and undertakers; all there were in town; he was going to have cavalry and artillery to put down the riots—amongst the people that couldn't get in. And he sent out invitations to all the celebrated people in America, and said he was going to seat them on the platform—when they came. He was going to have Senator Nye introduce me.

During three days I led the most exciting life I had ever known—and the happiest and proudest. Then I began to sober a little. It seemed to me that the excitement was too local—it didn't seem to be spreading outside of our quarters. I said so to Fuller. He said, Sho, the town is just boiling, underneath. Vesuvius! he said; that's what it is; and there's going to be an irruption—the biggest since Pompeii was buried. Don't fret—it's all right.

But the next three days were no better. The city was still calm; awfully calm; ominously calm, I feared. But Fuller was not troubled. He said there's always that kind of a calm before a storm. He said he was working the newspapers—keeping them quiet, so't they would begin to talk presently. Which they didn't. And he said they would talk after the lecture, too. I was afraid of that myself.

On the eighth day I was in a panic—for that deadly calm held on as solidly as ever. I couldn't hear a whisper anywhere about my lecture. Fuller said, don't worry—look at these; you'll see what these will do. They were little handbills the size of your hand, all display headings full of extravagant laudations of my celebrity and my lecture, and names of the illustrious people who were going to be there. He didn't say how many of them he had had printed, but there were 13 barrels of them. They were tied together in bunches of 50, with a string that had a loop to it. He had them hung up in the omnibuses and horse-cars, and also on all the door-knobs in town. I could not rest, I was too miserable, too distressed, too sad, too hopeless. I rode in omnibuses all that day, up and down Broadway, and watched those bunches of lies dangling from the cleats, crick in back of my neck from looking up, all day. But nobody ever took one; and gradually my heart broke. At least nobody took one till late in the afternoon. Then a man pulled one down and read it, and made me happy. His friend spoke up and asked Who is Mark Twain? and he said God knows—I don't.

These things seem funny, now, after 30 years; much funnier than they did then. But then the development of the humor of a thing is a pretty slow growth sometimes.

I did not ride any more. I went to Fuller and said the case is absolutely desperate. There isn't going to be a soul at the lecture—you must paper the house—you must load up every bench in it with dead-head tickets.

It made him sad to hear me talk so. He said "there *was* going to be $3,000 in it and $40,000 outside trying to get in—but your comfort is the first thing to be considered, and it shall be as you say. And I will give you the very best and brainiest dead-head audience that ever sat down under a roof in *this* world—both sexes, and every last one of them a schoolteacher." And straightway he began to send out market-baskets loaded with dead-head tickets. He fairly snowed the public schools under with them, north, south and west for 30 miles around New York. Then I felt better.

On the ninth and tenth days, we began to hear from the illustrious men who had been invited.

[A succession on the screen, here, of good portraits of the time, beginning with Grant and ending with Nye—with explanations of why they couldn't be present. Then portraits of the time, of Fuller and me. Then of us as at present; and then or at the end Fuller must come on and say he noticed, as I went along, that some of the things I said were true.]

The lecture was to begin at 8. I was nervous, and I went a little early. It was just as well that I did. Massed in the street were all the school teachers in America, apparently, and more coming. The streets were blocked, all traffic was at a standstill. It took me a while to get in. At 8 every seat was occupied. Even the huge stage was packed, and I never had a better time in my life. Fuller had kept his word: there were more brains there than were ever under a roof before—and without counting me.

And also, in the box-office, in cold cash, there was $35. First I began and worked up to and told Bucking horse—man got up—

I don't know what that wild scheme cost Fuller. He has

never mentioned the matter once. And when the newspaper notices came out in the morning he was the best satisfied man in New York. He said "You're a made man—you'll see." And just there comes the strangest part of it; just there this discredited prophet spoke true. Those notices went about the country, and lyceums that didn't know me from Adam began to shout for me to come. I responded—with modesty, but also with promptness. I accepted a hundred invitations at $100 a piece; and but for Fuller I wouldn't have been worth fourteen.

.   .   .

Well, Fuller's final idea was to invite the Queen of England. I said that that was nonsense; he said it *wasn't* nonsense. He said it was a good move; she wouldn't come, but no matter, the fact that she was invited would be published all over the world and would at once lift this show high up in the estimation of all mankind and make it respectable. And he wanted me to write the letter. Of course I refused. How little I imagined, at that time, that some day I should really be corresponding with the Queen of England. But we never can tell what is going to happen to us in this world—not even in the next. I did write her a letter—it was about 10 or 12 years ago. I didn't get any answer, because the mails were very irregular then; and so I didn't keep up the correspondence; but I did have the honor of writing her one letter, anyway. The way it happened was this. About 10 or 12 years ago

* * *

[AFTER GRANT—THIS.]

* * *

That anecdote about Gen. Grant's remark at Chicago, is in a sort of kinship with another remark evincing memory high-placed—a remark which was made to me in Europe 3 or 4 years ago by a Personage whose name, like Grant's, is widely known in the world.

* * *

[PICTURE OF PRINCE OF WALES.]

* * *

There he is—the Heir to one of the best positions that I know of. It so happened that ten or twelve years ago I was surprised and shocked to receive from England—from the Internal Revenue Office—a tax-bill of £48—an income-tax bill, levied on my English copyrights. I was shocked, but it was not all shock. I was flattered as well as shocked; flattered to be formally taken notice of by a foreign government. It seemed to kind of introduce me into the family of nations; seemed—well, it seemed to sort of recognize me as one of the Friendly Powers—not on a large scale, of course—not like Russia and China and those, but on a—well, on a secondary scale—New Jersey. Not one of the Six Powers, you understand, but No. 7. Not an actual *member* of the Concert of Europe, but a kind of understudy, in case one of them should get sick. So, really there was more pleasure than shock about it. Consequently, so as to *clinch* that thing—so that they couldn't get out of it, some time or other when there was a war breeding and I should want to come in and take a hand and help plan out the way to conduct it—I wrote over to the publisher not to make any protest; keep quiet, don't say anything, just pay the bill. And he did. And so to this day, just by that neat little turn, I am still one of the Seven Powers—sleeping-partner in the firm—and in those European affairs I can give advice whenever I want to. I've done it often. I don't get anything for it, and I don't get any answer, and don't want any. I only just want my advice followed—that's all—and I can see by the Cretan business that they've been doing it.

Yes, that part of that tax matter was all right, and flattering, but there was one feature of it that was less so—and *that* was, the *class* of industries under which the British Government had taxed my literary faculty. In England, everything is taxed in detail and *named;* and my publisher had advised me not to pay this tax because authors' copyright is nowhere named in the tax lists—it isn't mentioned at all. Still, I made him pay it, but I asked the British Government to tell me what head I came under. The Government sent me the vast printed document where every taxable thing under the sun was named, and most courteously explained that I was taxed under paragraph No. 14, section D. Now you will never believe it, but I give you my honor that this—*this*, which you see before you—was actually taxed as a Gas Works. If I have never spoken the truth before I have spoken it this time.

Well, even I, hurt as I was, was able to see that there was a sort of diabolical humor about that situation; and so, as Harper's Magazine wanted a squib about that time, I dug it out of that tax-bill. I put it in the form of a letter to the Queen of England—the rambling and garrulous letter of a pleasant and well-disposed and ignorant ass who had the idea that she conducted all the business of the Empire herself, and that the best way to get my literature taxed under some other head than Gas Works was to ask her to attend to it personally. It was a long letter, and I began by *explaining* why I came to her with the matter. I said "I do not know the people in the Inland Revenue Office, your majesty, and it is embarrassing to me to correspond with strangers; for I was raised in the country and have always lived there, the early part in Marion county,

Missouri, before the War, and this part in Hartford county, Connecticut, near Bloomfield and about 8 miles this side of Farmington, though some call it 9, which it is impossible to be, for I have walked it many and many a time in considerably under 3 hours, and General Hawley says he has done it in 2¼, which is not likely; so it seemed best that I write your Majesty. It is true that I do not know your Majesty personally, but I have met the Lord Mayor, and if the rest of the Family are like him, it is but just that it should be named royal; and likewise plain that in a family matter like this I cannot better forward my case than to frankly carry it to the head of the family itself. I have also met the Prince of Wales once, in the fall of 1873, but it was not in any familiar way, but in a quite informal way,—being casual—and was of course a surprise to us both. It was in Oxford street, just where you come out of Oxford into Regent Circus, over there, you know, where the hat store is, a little above where that corner grocery used to be, you remember, and just as the Prince turned up one side of the circle at the head of a Sons of Temperance procession, I went down the other on the top of a bus. He will remember me on account of a light gray coat with flap pockets that I wore, as I was the only person on the omnibus that had on that kind of a coat; and I remember him of course as easy as I would a comet. He looked quite proud and satisfied, but that is not to be wondered at, as he has a good situation. And once I called on your Majesty, but they said you were out. But that is no matter, it happens with everybody. I will call again.

Of course, your Majesty, my idea was that this tax that I am coming to was for only about 1 percent., but last night I met Professor Sloane, professor of history at Princeton University and *he* said it was 2½.

.   .   .

[PICTURE OF SLOANE]

.   .   .

You may not know Mr. Sloane, but you have probably seen him every now and then, for he goes to England a good deal—a large man and very handsome and absorbed in thought, and if you have noticed such a man on platforms after the train is gone, that is the one, he generally gets left; for he is like all those historians and specialists and scholars, they know everything except how to apply it."

And so on and so on and so on. It was a very long letter, and very intelligent; and by and by got down to the subject, and explained it. I wish I had the rest of the letter here, to read it, and I wish I had the answer to it that miscarried, I would read that, too; because I like to talk about it, and it always makes me proud to remember that I have corresponded with a Queen, for very few people have had a distinction like that. It's a fascinating thing to talk about,—however, I've got to move along, I reckon.

Well, Fuller was bound that the Prince of Wales should be invited to the lecture; and maybe he did invite him—I never knew—I remember—I remember he didn't come.

.   .   .

[PICTURE OF THE PRINCE]

.   .   .

So at last I consented. Well, I couldn't well resist when he said he was going to have all the distinguished people in the country at the lecture—that conquered me—it made me feel good—and proud. Yes, he had buttered me in the right place. He said he was going to have Nasby.

.   .   .

[PICTURE OF NASBY.]

.   .   .

Now *there* was a good fellow. He was sweeping the country with his lecture, "Cursed by Canaan," in those days—packing his houses to the ceiling. He told me once that in his first campaign he delivered that lecture during a stretch of 9 straight months without ever missing a night. Yet he always read it from MS. He wouldn't trust his memory for a single sentence. Not because he hadn't a good memory, but because he hadn't any confidence in it. The lecture began, "We are all descended from grandfathers;" and he said that when the terrible 9 months were over he went home and slept 3 days and nights, with only 3 little breaks—momentary breaks—at 8 o'clock—lecture-time—each night. Then he woke up and said "We are all descended from grandfathers," and went to sleep again. Force of habit. And Fuller would have Josh Billings at my lecture.

.   .   .

[PICTURE OF JOSH.]

.   .   .

Another good fellow—good as ever was. He too was a great card on the lecture platform in those days; and his quaint and pithy maxims were on everybody's tongue. He said "Some folks mistake vivacity for wit; whereas the difference between vivacity and wit is the same as the difference between the lightning-bug and the lightning." And he said, "*Don't* take the bull by the horns, take him by the tail, and then you can let go when you want to." Also he said, "The difficulty ain't that we know so much, but that we know so much that ain't so." Good friends of mine, he and Nasby were. Good fellows, too, and have gone the way that all the good fellows go. Yes, and Anna Dickinson would be at my lecture, too—

. . .

[PICTURE OF ANNA.]

. . .

My, what houses she used to draw! Some of you remember those determined lips and those indignant eyes, and how they used to snap and flash when she marched the platform pouring out the lava of her blistering eloquence upon the enemy. But that old platform is desolate, now—nobody left on it but me. And Horace Greeley was to be at my lecture, too.

. . .

[PICTURE OF HIM.]

. . .

He was a great man, an honest man, and served his country well, and was an honor to it. Also he was a good-hearted man, but abrupt with strangers if they annoyed him when he was busy. He was profane, but that is nothing—the best of us is that, thank goodness. I did not know him well—but only just casually, and by accident. I never met him but once. I called on him in the Tribune office, but I was not intending to. I was looking for Whitelaw Reid and got into the wrong den. He was alone, at his desk writing, and we conversed—not long, but just a little. I asked him if he was well, and he said "What the hell do *you* want?" Well—I couldn't remember what I wanted, and so I said I would call again. But I didn't. And Fuller said we would have Oliver W. Holmes.

∘   ∘   ∘

[PICTURE OF HIM.]

∘   ∘   ∘

He was a good friend of mine, and wrote me a poem on my 50th birth-day. I plagiarized the dedication of one of his books and used it in the Innocents Abroad. I didn't know I had plagiarized him, but a friend proved it to me. I told Dr. Holmes about it and it made us good friends. He said we were all plagiarists, consciously or *un*consciously, one or the other. It made me feel good to be one or the other—but he didn't say *which*.

∘   ∘   ∘

ISSUING THE INVITATIONS.

GRANT.

There—that is the greatest man I have ever had the privilege of knowing personally. And I have not known a man with a kinder nature or a purer character. He was called the Silent Man—the Sphynx—and he was that, in public, but not in private. There he was a fluent and able talker—with a large sense of humor, and a most rare gift of compacting meaty things into phrases of stunning felicity—such as those which he used to flash out from his campaigns and send flying abroad over the globe—"Will fight it out on this line if it takes all summer."

Along with his other great gifts he had that rare sort of memory—the memory which remembers names and faces. [Anecdote.]

I published his book—I say I, because I was the bulk of the firm of Charles L. Webster & Co, publishers. That is, I furnished the money, not the brains. Nobody furnished the brains. The book published itself—it was strong enough to go alone—it needed no help.

The last time I saw Gen. Grant alive was a few days before his death. He knew that his end was very near. He was sitting in his chair, fully dressed; his book was finished, and he was putting one or two finishing touches to it with his pencil—the last work he was ever to do. He had been for some time in very straightened circumstances,—had lost everything he had in the world through the depredations of the infamous firm which had not only reduced him to penury but had brought shame and humiliation upon him, and now all his solicitude was for his family—he had written his book solely that they might not be left in the grip of hard fortune when he was gone. He had said when he first began to write the book that he hoped it would realize as much as General Sherman's memoirs had produced; he said that that was $25,000, and he would be satisfied with that. He asked me if I thought his book would do as well. And now at death's door the thought of his family was at his heart and he came back to that matter once more; and he wrote a question on his tablets, Could I give him an idea this early of how much the book might yield? He wrote because he could not speak. The cancer in his throat had done its work—in intolerable pain the book had been written—month after month it had been a day and night race between the soldier and death— the grave was in sight, now, but the soldier who had never lost a fight had won. He had won, but he had to ask his question with his pencil, for the voice had fallen silent which had said so many inspiring things when the clouds hung low upon the spirits of his countrymen, and the voice which had never failed in its uplifting office since the day that it first made itself heard in the country's struggle for its life—that day that it dictated those words that revealed to this nation that there was a *man* risen up at the front, and that the day of vacillation and timidity and compromise was at an end in at least *one* of the country's thousand camps—"the only terms are—unconditional surrender."

. . .

[PICTURE OF GRANT SITTING IN HIS WRAPS. GET IT FROM THE ENGRAVING IN THE "CENTURY."] HOUSE *RISE.*

. . .

MUSIC.

. . .

But we do not need to lament for him. He did his mighty work, he died his noble death, and his name will live forever.

. . .

[PICTURE OF TOMB.]

. . .

I could answer his question without guessing. I already knew. I told him that his profit upon the orders already sent in by the General Agents and secured by safe bonds, would be $320,000. He was satisfied. As it turned out, his share of the profits was far and away beyond that. My firm's cash profit was $130,000; but by tact, perseverance, watchfulness and sagacity in discovering the right opportunities during 18 careful months they managed to waste it all and get in debt. Eighteen months. As a financial achievement, by people entirely unacquainted with finance, it does not need to hang its head in the presence of anything of the kind that has happened in the American history of that great science.

By continued caution, tact, watchfulness and inspired financiering, during the next 7 years, the firm was able to retire from business in debt—if my wife and I may be counted in with the other creditors—in debt $208,000 above the assets. However, my wife and I don't have to be paid, so that reduces the debt a good deal more than half. Nothing has to be paid but the rest of the debt; and here I stand, nobly paying it—out of your pockets. That is the way with debts; they just dump along, from shoulder to shoulder, and you never know who has got to foot the bill at last.

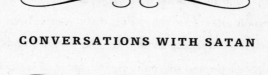

CONVERSATIONS WITH SATAN

I t was being whispered around that Satan was in Vienna
incognito, and the thought came into my mind that it
would be a great happiness to me if I could have the privilege of
interviewing him. "When you think of the Devil" he appears,
you know. It was past midnight, I was standing at the window
of my work-room high aloft on the third floor of the hotel,
and was looking down upon a stage-setting which is always
effective and impressive at that late hour: the great vacant
stone-paved square of the Morzin Platz with its sleeping file
of cab-horses and drivers counterfeiting the stillness and solemnity of death; and beyond the square a broad Milky Way
of innumerable lamps bending around the far-reaching curve
of the Donau canal, with not a suggestion of life or motion

visible anywhere under that glinting belt from end to end. If the square and the curve were dim or dark, the impressiveness would be wanting; but the multitudinous lights seem to belong properly with life and energy and the roar and tumult of traffic, and these being now wholly absent, the resulting impression conveyed to the spirit is that they have been suddenly and mysteriously annihilated, and that this brooding midnight silence and solemnity are the signs and symbols of the tragedy that has happened.

Now, with a most strange suddenness came an inky darkness, with a stormy rush of wind, a crash of thunder and a glare of lightning; and the glare vividly revealed the figure of a slender and shapely gentleman in black coming leisurely across the empty square. By his dress he was an Anglican Bishop; but I noticed that he cast a shadow. That gave him away, as Goethe phrases it; for by the ministrations of lightning no legitimate Anglican Bishop can do that—nor can any other earth-born creature, for that matter. This person was Satan. I knew it. It was in his honor that the sudden storm had been summoned and its thunders delivered in salute. It was inspiring, it was uplifting, this sublime ceremonial. If I had been a monarch it would have spoiled, for one while, my satisfaction in my little artillery salutes. And yet I would have tried to be properly philosophical, and ease and content myself with the

reflection that the honors had been fairly and justly propor-
tioned to the difference existing between Satan's importance
and mine, I being but a passing and evanescent master of a
limited patch of empire, and he the long-term master of the
majority of the human race.

I had that glimpse of Satan and his shadow, and the next
moment he was by my side in the room. He did not embarrass me. Real royalties do not embarrass one; they are sure
of their place, sure of its recognition; and so they bear about
with them an alpine serenity and reposefulness which quiet
the nerves of the spectator. It is the prerogative of a viscount
or a baron to make a person feel small, and of a baronet to
extinguish him.

Satan would not allow me to take his hat, but put it on the
table himself, and begged me not to put myself to any trouble
about him, but treat him just as I would an old friend; and
added that that was what he was—an old friend of mine, and
also one of my most ardent and grateful admirers. It seemed a
doubtful compliment; still, it was said in such a winning and
gracious way that I could not help feeling gratified and proud.
His carriage and manners were enviably fine and courtly, and
he was a handsome person, with delicate white hands and an
intellectual face and that subtle air of distinction which goes
with ancient blood and high lineage, commanding position

and habitual intercourse with the choicest society. The usual portraits of him are but resemblances, nothing more. They are very inaccurate. None of them is recent. The latest is as much as three hundred years old. They were all made by monks, and from memory; for the monks did not tarry. The monk was always excited, and he put his excitement into the picture. He thus conveyed an error, for Satan is a calm person; aristocratically calm and self-possessed. Satan's face is notably intellectual, and fine, and expressive. It suggests Don Quixotte's, and also Richelieu's, but it is not so melancholy as the one nor so austere as the other; and neither of those grand faces has the winning quality which is the immortal charm and grace of Satan's.

In Germany the sofa is the seat of honor and is always offered to the guest. It may be so in Austria also, therefore I tendered it to Satan, and called him by the loftiest titles I could think of—*Durchlauchtigst,* and *Ihre Majestät*—but he declined it, saying he would have no ceremony, and so took a chair. He said—

"You are very comfortable here. The German stove is the best in the universe."

"I agree to that, with all my heart, Durchlaucht. That one there is eleven feet high and four feet square, and looks like a graveyard monument built of white tiles; but its looks are its only blemish. At eight in the morning it burns up one small basketful of wood in twenty minutes, and that is all it requires for the day. This great room will keep the same level and pleasant and comfortable degree of warmth hour after hour without change, and there is no artificial heat in the world that is comparable to it for wholesomeness, healthfulness. It does not inflame the skin, it does not oppress the head or make the temples throb; there isn't a headache in a hundred years of it. As for economy, it is a good ten times more economical than any other house-heating apparatus known to the world."

"You use it in America, of course?"

I was pleasantly surprised at that, and said—

"Is it possible that Ihre Majestät is not familiar with America?"

"Well—no. I have not been there lately. I am not needed there."

At first I was gratified; but next I was suspicious that maybe his remark did not quite mean what I had thought it meant; so it seemed good diplomacy not to stir the matter, but leave it alone and go on about the stove again.

"No," I said, "we don't use the German stove in America. We have the name of being the most ingenious of the nations in the matter of inventing and putting to practical use all manner of conveniences, comforts, and labor-saving and money-saving contrivances, and we have fairly earned that name and are proud of it; but we do not know how to heat a house rationally, yet, and it seems likely that we shall never learn. The most of our stoves are extravagant wasters of fuel; the most of them require frequent attention and recharging; none of them furnishes a continuously equable heat, and we have not one that does not scorch the skin and oppress the head. We have spent tons and tons of money upon furnaces with elaborate and costly arrangements for distributing dry heat or steam or hot water throughout a house; but they are all ravenous coal-cannibals, and if there is one among them whose heat-output can be successfully regulated I have not seen it. As far as my knowledge goes, we have none but insane ways of heating houses and railway cars in America."

"Then why don't you introduce the German stove?"

"I wish I could. I could save the country money enough annually to pay the silly pension bill. And if we had that admirable stove we should soon find a way to rid it of its grim and ghostly look and make it a pretty and graceful thing to look at, and an ornament to the room; for we are a capable people in those directions. But I suppose we shall never see the day. The Americans who come over here do not study the German stove, they merely make fun of its personal appearance, and go away without finding out what a competent and inexpensive miracle it is. The Berlin stove is the best that I have seen. When we kept house there several winters ago we charged our parlor monument at 7 in the morning with a peck of cheap briquettes made of refuse coal-dust, let the fire burn half an hour, then shut up the stove and never touched it again for twenty-four hours. All day long and up to past midnight that room was perfectly comfortable, not too hot, not too cold, and the heat not varying, but remaining at the same pleasant level all the time. Do you like the German stove, Durchlaucht?"

"Not for my boarders—no."

"What do you use, Durchlaucht?"

He named sixty-four varieties of stoves and house-furnaces. Dear me, those old familiar names—they were all American! But I didn't say anything. I was ashamed; and yet at the same time I was conscious of a private little thrill of patriotic pride in the reflection that in a humble way we had been able to add a discomfort to hell.

Of course we were smoking, all this time, for Durchlaucht has had experience of the chief joy of man for many ages. The early American Indians introduced it in Sheol twenty or thirty thousand years ago, and out of gratitude he is never severe on that race. I thought I would venture to indicate in an unobtrusive way that by rights I was an Indian, though changed in the cradle through no fault of mine—and waited timorously for a comment. But I was disappointed. He only looked. It may be that he did not mean anything by the look, but often a look like that is discouraging, anyway, if you are conscious yourself that you have been trying to pull a person's leg, as the saying is. In such cases you let on that you did not know you had said anything; and it is the best way, and soonest over.

Then you change the subject; and I did. I asked him to try the Navy Cut, and I loaded his pipe with it and gave him a light. He liked it. I was sure he would. He sent up a cloud of fragrant smoke, and said admiringly—

"It is good; very, very good; burns freely and smells like a heretic."

That made me shudder a little, but that was nothing; we all have our metaphors, symbols, figures of speech, and they vary according to habitat, environment, taste, training, and so on.

"Where do you get this tobacco?"

"In London, Durchlaucht."

"But where in Vienna?"

"It is a pity to have to say it, but one can't get it in Vienna at all."

"You must be mistaken about that. You must remember that this is one of the most superb cities that was ever built; and is very rich, and very fond of good things, and can command the best of everything that the world can furnish; and it also has the disposition to do it. This is my favorite city. I was its patron saint in the early times before the reorganization of things, and I still have much influence here, and am greatly respected. When you intimate that there is anything of first excellence which one cannot get in Vienna, you hurt my feelings. You would not wish to hurt my feelings?"

"I? Indeed, no. Do not look at me like that, Durchlaucht; you break my heart. But what I have said is really the truth. Consider what this noble city smokes—latakia! It is true, just as I say. It smokes latakia, and fine-cut Turkish and Syrian ordure that burns your tongue and makes a mephitic odor which suffocates."

We are a vain and thoughtless race. In criticising in this large and arrogant way other people's tastes in the matter of tobacco I was satirizing myself, without for the moment being conscious of it. For it has been my habit to look down in a superior way upon persons who were so low in the scale of intelligence as to believe such a thing possible as the establishing of a *standard* of excellence in tobacco and cigars. Tastes in this matter seem to be infinite. Each man seems to have a standard of his own, and he also seems to be ashamed of the next man's taste and hostile to his standard. I think that no one's standard is steadfast, but is at all times open to change. When we travel, and are obliged to go without our favorite brand and take up with the cigar of the country we chance to be in, we presently find ourselves establishing *that* cigar as our standard. In Venice we are at first too good to smoke those cheap black rat-tail "Virginias" that have a straw through them, but a fortnight's familiarity with them changes all that and we adopt the Virginia as our standard. In Florence and Rome we are sorry for a people who are condemned to smoke the cheap menghettis and trabucos, but soon we prefer them to any other cigars. In Germany, France and Switzerland we take less kindly to the native cigars; but in India we quickly come to believe that the Madras two-cent cigar is much better than the Cuban cigar which costs twenty cents in New York. I must not claim to speak fairly and justly about high-priced cigars, for I have never bought any myself, and have not smoked other people's when I could substitute a cheap one of my own without being discovered; for to my mind there is no cigar that is quite so vile and stenchy and inflammable as a twenty-cent Havana. This is probably a superstition; for I am well satisfied that all notions, of whatever sort, concerning cigars, are superstitions—superstitions and stupidities, and nothing else. It distresses me to hear an otherwise sane man talk about "good" cigars, and pretend to know what a good cigar is—as if by any chance his standard could be a standard for anybody else.

We have all noticed this—and it tells its own story: that when we go out to dine at another man's house, we privately carry along a handful of cigars as a protection. We know that the chances are that his standard and ours will differ. We take his cigar, but we manage a substitution furtively. From long habit—backed by prejudice and superstition—I dread those high-priced Havanas with a fancy label around them; a label which costs the hundredth part of a cent, and augments the price of the cigar twenty-seven degrees beyond its value. I have accepted tons of those; and given them to the poor. It is not that I hate the poor, for I do not; but only because I cannot bring myself to waste anything, even a fancy-labeled execrable cigar.

Not more than two persons in eight hundred thousand know even their own cigars when they are outside of the box; they think they do, but that is another superstition. Years ago several friends of mine used to come to my house every Friday night to play billiards. They patiently smoked my cheap cigars and never said a wounding word about them. With one exception. That was a gentleman who thought he knew all about cigars, and whose opinion was like the rest of the world's—not valuable. He had a high-priced brand of his own, and he did not like my cheap weeds. He tried to smoke them, but he growled all the time, and always threw the cigar away after a few whiffs, and tried another and another and another. He did that all one winter. The truth was, that they were his own cigars, not mine. By request, his wife sent me a couple of dozen every Friday afternoon. He may not believe this when he sees it in print, but the other witnesses are there yet, and they will confirm the truth of my statement.

And I have another case. One winter, along in those years, I heard that the "long nine" of fifty years ago was being manufactured and marketed again, and I was glad, for I had smoked them when I was a lad of nine or ten and knew that twelve or fifteen of them could be depended upon to make a day pass pleasantly at light cost. I sent to Wheeling and laid in a supply, at 27 cents a barrel. They were delightful. But their personal appearance was distinctly against them; and besides they came in boxes that were not attractive; boxes that held a hundred each and were made of coarse blue pasteboard; boxes that were crazy, and battered, and caved in, and ugly and vulgar and plebian, and looked like the nation. Just the aspect of the box itself would make anybody sea-sick but me; with the burnt-rag aspect of its homely contents added, the result was truly formidable.

I could not venture to offer these things, undisguised, to my friends, for I had no desire to be shot; so I put fancy labels around a lot of them, and kept them in a polished mahogany box with a perforated false bottom that had a damp sponge under it; and gave them a large Spanish name which nobody could spell but myself and no ignorant person could pronounce; and said that these cigars were a present to me from the Captain General of Cuba, and were not procurable for money at any price. These simple devices were successful. My friends contemplated the long nines with the deepest reverence, and smoked them the whole evening in an ecstasy of happiness, and went away grateful to me and with their souls steeped in a sacred joy.

I carried the experiment no further, but dropped it there. A year later these same men were at my house to discuss a topic of some sort—for it was a social club, and its members met fortnightly at each other's houses in the winter time, and discussed questions of the day, and finished with a late supper and much smoking. This time, in the midst of the supper, the colored waiter came to me, looking as pale as amber, and whispered and said he had forgotten to provide proper cigars, and there was no substitute in the house but the vulgar long nines in the blue pasteboard boxes—what should he do? I said pass them around and say nothing—we could not help ourselves at this late hour. He passed them.

It was usual for these people to smoke and talk an hour and a half. But this time they did not do that. They looked at the battered blue box dubiously, and in turn took out a long nine hesitatingly, and lit it. Then an uncanny silence fell upon the company; conversation died. Then, after five minutes, a man excused himself and left—had an engagement, he said. In a couple of minutes, another man lied himself out. Within ten minutes the whole twelve were gone and I was alone; and it was not yet eleven o'clock.

In the morning at breakfast the colored man asked me how far it was from the front door to the upper gate. I said it was a hundred and twenty-five feet. Then he said, impressively, "Well, sir, you can walk the whole way, and step on a long nine every time."

What an exposure of human nature it is. Those were the same cigars that had lifted those people into heaven a year before. They had smoked all their lives, yet they knew nothing about cigars. The only way that they could tell a fine cigar from a poor one was by the label and the box; and the great majority of men are just like them. The wine merchant and the cigar dealer have an easy chance to get rich, for it is merely a matter of knowing how to select the right labels.

In the continental States, tobacco is a government monopoly, and the tobacco used is native—almost altogether. In Vienna there is but one shop where importations can be had. But it keeps no endurable brands of English or American smoking tobacco. When I speak of English tobacco I mean American tobacco manufactured in England. America has many brands of good smoking tobacco; and could have good and cheap native cigars, I suppose. In fact we had good native cigars fifteen years ago, but none now, so far as I know. I am not hard to please, but to my mind the American native cigar is easily the worst in the world—and it costs from seven to ten cents, too. The trabuco cigar, furnished by the Austrian government, suits my taste exactly, comes up to my strictest standard, and even a little above it; and it costs just 40 cents a hundred. The best native American cigar cannot compare with it. Perhaps it is our high protection that has degraded our tobacco. There being no foreign competition, we can compel ninety-nine Americans in the hundred to smoke any rubbish we please, since he cannot afford the imported article; and as a result we are the only considerable nation in the world which smokes supremely villainous cigars.

Possibly my approval of the Austrian cigar pays it but a doubtful compliment, but I do not think so. For I am one of the sixteen men now alive in the world who estimate a cigar by its personal qualities, not by its name and its price.

JANE AUSTEN

Whenever I take up "Pride and Prejudice" or "Sense and Sensibility," I feel like a barkeeper entering the Kingdom of Heaven. I mean, I feel as he would probably feel, would almost certainly feel. I am quite sure I know what his sensations would be—and his private comments. He would be certain to curl his lip, as those ultra-good Presbyterians went filing self-complacently along. Because he considered himself better than they? Not at all. They would not be to his *taste*—that is all.

He would not want to associate with them; he would not like their gait, their style, their ways; their talk would enrage him. Yet he would be secretly ashamed of himself, secretly angry with himself that this was so. Why? Because barkeepers are like everybody else—it humiliates them to find that there are fine things, great things, admirable things, which others can perceive and they can't.

What would the barkeeper do next? Give it up and go down below, where his own kind are? No, not yet. He would wander out into the solitudes and take a long rest; then he would brace up and attack the proposition again, saying to himself, "others have found the secret charm that is in those Presbyterians, therefore it must be a fact, and not an illusion; I will try again; what those others have found, I can find."

So he tries again. Does he succeed? No. Because he has not educated his taste yet, he has not reformed his taste, his taste remains as it was before, and the thing involved is purely a matter of *taste:* he will not be able to enjoy those Presbyterians until he has learned to admire them.

Does Jane Austen do her work too remorselessly well? For me, I mean? Maybe that is it. She makes me detest all her people, without reserve. Is that her intention? It is not believable. Then is it her purpose to make the reader detest her people up to the middle of the book and like them in the rest of the chapters? That could be. That would be high art. It would be worth while, too. Some day I will examine the other end of her books and see.

All the great critics praise her art generously. To start

with, they say she draws her characters with sharp discrimination and a sure touch. I believe that this is true, as long as the characters she is drawing are odious. I am doing "Sense and Sensibility" now, and have accomplished the first third of it—not for the first time. To my mind, Marianne is not attractive; I am sure I should not care for her, in actual life. I suppose she was intended to be unattractive. Edward Ferrars has fallen in love with Elinor, and she with him; the justification of this may develop later, but thus far there is no way to account for it; for, thus far, Elinor is a wax figure and Edward a shadow, and how could such manufactures as these warm up and feel a passion. Edward is an unpleasant shadow, because he has discarded his harmless waxwork and engaged himself to Lucy Steele, who is coarse, ignorant, vicious, brainless, heartless, a flatterer, a sneak—and is described by the supplanted waxwork as being "a woman superior in person and understanding to half her sex;" and "time and habit will teach Edward to forget that he ever thought another superior to her." Elinor knows Lucy quite well. Are those sentimental falsities put into her mouth to make us think she is a noble and magnanimous waxwork, and thus exalt her in our estimation? And do they do it?

Willoughby is a frankly cruel, criminal and filthy society-gentleman.

Old Mrs. Ferrars is an execrable gentlewoman and unsurpassably coarse and offensive.

Mr. Dashwood, gentleman, is a coarse and cold-hearted money-worshipper; his Fanny is coarse and mean. Neither of them ever says or does a pleasant thing.

Mr. Robert Ferrars, gentleman, is coarse, is a snob, and an all-round offensive person.

Mr. Palmer, gentleman, is coarse, brute-mannered, and probably an ass, though we cannot tell, yet, because he cloaks himself behind silences which are not often broken by speeches that contain material enough to construct an analysis out of.

His wife, lady, is coarse and silly.

Lucy Steele's sister is coarse, foolish, and disagreeable.

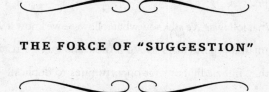

THE FORCE OF "SUGGESTION"

If a wave of incendiarism were sweeping the country from the Atlantic to the Pacific and from the lakes to the Gulf, and you knew the names and addresses of every one of the incendiaries, what would you do—double the strength of the 2,000 fire departments?

That would be one way. Another would be, to put the incendiaries under bonds to stop setting fires.

"Suggestion," as an impelling and compelling force, is not confined to the hypnotist—the most of our daily acts proceed from it. If a newspaper tells of a starving family, the bare suggestion is sufficient, it does not need to solicit help for it, the donations will begin to flow in, without that; if a newspaper tells of a child that has been abandoned by its parents, there is no need to ask for succor, fifty childless homes are eagerly flung open for the waif; if a newspaper gathers from the police court the inflaming particulars of how a young girl has been captured in a lonely place by one or a dozen ruffians and outraged—

What follows? We all know what follows—we know it well: the inflaming particulars excite a thousand ruffian readers, and they frenziedly hunt for opportunities to duplicate that crime.

If the published case be very liberally spiced with salacious particulars, the 2,000 daily journals of the United States will print it, and some hundreds of thousands of ruffians will be set on fire by it, driven temporarily insane by it, rendered practically irresponsible by it; and while this frenzy lasts they will take the most desperate chances to duplicate that crime.

How many attempts that fall short of complete success will ensue? Certainly hundreds upon hundreds that will be hushed up and never heard of—because the parents cannot get private justice, but must carry their shame into a public court and have it laid bare to the world—the newspapers, and the pictures of themselves and their ruined child along with it. If the case were yours would you carry it to the public court and the newspaper? Would I? No. We would suffer any death first.

How many successes reach the courts? One in a hundred? Possibly; but not any more than that. How many unsuccessful attempts reach the courts? One in ten thousand? Possibly; but not any more than that.

When a drinker is trying to reform, we hasten to put the bottle out of sight when he enters our house—for we know the transcendent force of suggestion; when the gambler is trying to reform we keep the cards out of his sight; the law closes the mails against salacious books, lest they get into the hands of the young and undermine their morals. Then—isn't it strange!—we open the mails every day to 2,000 newspapers, and privilege them to incite the impressible young, and many evil-minded adults among millions of readers, to think poisonous thoughts, and imagine unwholesome scenes and episodes, and meditate deeds perilous to themselves and to society. And to this unwisdom we add the public court, and thus do our very best to utterly complete the debauching of the public mind, and at the same time totally defeat certain of the very ends for which the courts have been established.

The present "wave of crime" is a perfectly natural thing. It was created by the open court and the newspaper. This result was unavoidable. So long as the court remains open it will be the newspaper's business to print the cases, and it will be obliged to do it.

I think it likely that if for a couple of months the cases were examined in secret and kept out of the newspapers—this by way of experiment—the "wave" would quiet down, the heated ruffian mind would cool off, and crimes against women and girls would become practically infrequent.

We know one thing for sure: five million policemen could not abolish this wave, in America, nor even modify it. These crimes are not committed in the presence of policemen.

MARK TWAIN

THE PRIVILEGE OF THE GRAVE

Its occupant has one privilege which is not exercised by any living person: free speech. The living man is not really without this privilege—strictly speaking—but as he possesses it merely as an empty formality, and knows better than to make use of it, it cannot be seriously regarded as an actual possession. As an active privilege, it ranks with the privilege of committing murder: we may exercise it if we are willing to take the consequences. Murder is forbidden both in form and in fact; free speech is granted in form but forbidden in fact. By the common estimate both are crimes, and are held in deep odium by all civilized peoples. Murder is sometimes punished, free speech always—*when* committed. Which is seldom. There are not fewer than five thousand murders to one (unpopular) free utterance. There is justification for this reluctance to utter unpopular opinions: the cost of utterance is too heavy; it can ruin a man in his business, it can lose him his friends, it can subject him to public insult and abuse, it can ostracise his unoffending family, and make his house a despised and unvisited solitude. An unpopular opinion concerning politics or religion lies concealed in the breast of every man; in many cases not only one sample, but several. The more intelligent the man, the larger the freightage of this kind of opinions he carries, and keeps to himself. There is not one individual—including the reader and myself—who is not the possessor of dear and cherished unpopular convictions which common wisdom forbids him to utter. Sometimes we suppress an opinion for reasons that are a credit to us, not a discredit, but oftenest we suppress an unpopular opinion because we cannot afford the bitter cost of putting it forth. None of us likes to be hated, none of us likes to be shunned.

A natural result of these conditions is, that we consciously or unconsciously pay more attention to tuning our opinions to our neighbor's pitch and preserving his approval than we do to examining the opinions searchingly and seeing to it that they are right and sound. This custom naturally produces another result: public opinion being born and reared on this plan, it is not opinion at all, it is merely *policy;* there is no reflection back of it, no principle, and is entitled to no respect.

When an entirely new and untried political project is sprung upon the people, they are startled, anxious, timid, and for a time they are mute, reserved, non-committal. The great majority of them are not studying the new doctrine and making up their minds about it, they are waiting to see which is going to be the popular side. In the beginning of the anti-slavery agitation three-quarters of a century ago, in the North, it found no sympathy there. Press, pulpit and nearly every-body blew cold upon it. This was from timidity—the fear of speaking out and becoming obnoxious; not from approval of slavery or lack of pity for the slave; for all nations like the State of Virginia and myself are not exceptions to this rule; we joined the Confederate cause not because we wanted to, for we did not, but we wanted to be in the swim. It is plainly a law of nature, and we obeyed it.

It is desire to be in the swim that makes successful political parties. There is no higher motive involved—with the major-ity—unless membership in a party because one's father was a member of it is one. The average citizen is not a student of party doctrines, and quite right: neither he nor I would ever be able to understand them. If you should ask him to *explain*—in intelligible detail—why he preferred one of the coin-standards to the other, his attempt to do it would be disgraceful. The same with the tariff. The same with any other large political doctrine; for all large political doctrines are rich in difficult problems—problems that are quite above the average citizen's reach. And that is not strange, since they are also above the reach of the ablest minds in the country; after all the fuss and all the talk, not one of those doctrines has been conclusively proven to be the right one and the best.

When a man has joined a party, he is likely to stay in it. If he change his opinion—his feeling, I mean, his sentiment—he is likely to stay, anyway; his friends are of that party, and he will keep his altered sentiment to himself, and talk the privately discarded one. On those terms he can exercise his American privilege of free speech, but not on any others. These unfortunates are in both parties, but in what proportions we cannot guess. Therefore we never know which party was really in the majority at an election.

Free speech is the privilege of the dead, the monopoly of the dead. They can speak their honest minds without offending. We have charity for what the dead say. We may disapprove of what they say, but we do not insult them, we do not revile them, as knowing they cannot now defend themselves. If they should speak, what revelations there would be! For it would be found that in matters of opinion no departed person was exactly what he had passed for in life; that out of fear, or out of calculated wisdom, or out of reluctance to wound friends, he had long kept to himself certain views not suspected by his little world, and had carried them unuttered to the grave. And then the living would be brought by this to a poignant and reproachful realization of the fact that they, too, were tarred by that same brush. They would realize, deep down, that they, and whole nations along with them, are not really what they seem to be—and never can be.

Now there is hardly one of us but would dearly like to reveal these secrets of ours; we know we cannot do it in life, then why not do it from the grave, and have the satisfaction of it? Why not put these things into our diaries, instead of so discreetly leaving them out? Why not put them in, and leave the diaries behind, for our friends to read? For free speech *is* a desirable thing. I felt it in London, five years ago, when Boer sympathisers—respectable men, tax payers, good citizens, and as much entitled to their opinions as were any other citizens—were mobbed at their meetings, and their speakers maltreated and driven from the platform by other citizens who differed from them in opinion. I have felt it in America when we have mobbed meetings and battered the speakers.

And most particularly I feel it every week or two when I want to print something that a fine discretion tells me I mustn't. Sometimes my feelings are so hot that I have to take to the pen and pour them out on paper to keep them from setting me afire inside; then all that ink and labor are wasted, because I can't print the result. I have just finished an article of this kind, and it satisfies me entirely. It does my weather-beaten soul good to read it, and admire the trouble it would make for me and the family. I will leave it behind, and utter it from the grave. There is free speech there, and no harm to the family.

MARK TWAIN

A GROUP OF SERVANTS

June 4, Kaltenleutgeben. In this family we are four. When a family has been used to a group of servants whose several terms of service with it cover these periods, to wit: 10 years, 12 years, 13 years, 17 years, 19 years, and 22 years, it is not able to understand the new ways of a new group straight off. That would be the case at home; abroad it is the case emphasized. We have been housekeeping a fortnight, now—long enough to have learned how to pronounce the servants' names, but not to spell them. We shan't ever learn to spell them; they were invented in Hungary and Poland, and on paper they look like the alphabet out on a drunk. There are four: two maids, a cook, and a middle-aged woman who comes once or twice a day to help around generally. They are good-natured and friendly, and capable and willing. Their ways are not the ways which we have been so long used to with the home tribe in America, but they are agreeable, and no fault is to be found with them except in one or two particulars. The cook is a love, but she talks at a gait and with a joyous interest and energy which make everything buzz. She is always excited; gets excited over big and little things alike, for she has no sense of proportion. Whether the project in hand is a barbecued bull or a handmade cutlet it is no matter, she loses her mind; she unlimbers her tongue, and while her breath holds out you can't tell her from a field day in the Austrian Parliament. But what of it, as long as she can cook? And she can do that. She has that mysterious art which is so rare in the world—the art of making everything taste good which comes under the enchantment of her hand. She is the kind of cook that establishes confidence with the first meal; establishes it so thoroughly that after that you do not care to know the materials of the dishes nor their names: that her hall-mark is upon them is sufficient.

The youngest of the two maids, Charlotte, is about twenty; strong, handsome, capable, intelligent, self-contained, quiet— in fact, rather reserved. She has character, and dignity.

The other maid, Wuthering Heights (which is not her name), is about forty and looks considerably younger. She is quick, smart, active, energetic, breezy, good-natured, has a high-keyed voice and a loud one, talks thirteen to the dozen, talks all the time, talks in her sleep, will talk when she is dead; is here, there, and everywhere all at the same time, and is consumingly interested in every devilish thing that is going on. Particularly if it is not her affair. And she is not merely passively interested, but takes a hand; and not only takes a hand but the principal one; in fact will play the whole game, fight the whole battle herself, if you don't find some way to turn her flank. But as she does it in the family's interest, not her own, I find myself diffident about finding fault. Not so the family. It gravels the family. I like that. Not maliciously, but because it spices the monotony to see the family graveled. Sometimes they are driven to a point where they are sure they cannot endure her any longer, and they rise in revolt; but I stand between her and harm, for I adore Wuthering Heights. She is not a trouble to me, she freshens up my life, she keeps me interested all the time. She is not monotonous, she does not stale, she is fruitful of surprises, she is always breaking out in a new place. The family are always training her, always caulking her, but it does not make me uneasy any more, now, for I know that as fast as they stop one leak she will spring another. Her talk is my circus, my menagerie, my fireworks, my spiritual refreshment. When she is at it I would rather be there than at a fire. She talks but little to me, for I understand only about half that she says, and I have had the sagacity not to betray that I understand that half. But I open my door when she is talking to the Executive at the other end of the house, and then I hear everything, and the enjoyment is without alloy, for it is like being at a show on a free ticket. She makes the Executive's head ache. I am sorry for that, of course; still it is a thing which cannot be helped. We must take things as we find them in this world.

The Executive's efforts to reconstruct Wuthering Heights are marked by wisdom, patience and gentle and persuasive speech. They will succeed, yet, and it is a pity. This morning at half past eight I was lying in my bed counterfeiting sleep; the Executive was lying in hers, reasoning with Wuthering Heights, who had just brought the hot water and was buzzing around here and there and yonder preparing the baths and putting all manner of things to rights with her lightning touch, and accompanying herself with a torrent of talk, cramped down to a low-voiced flutter to keep from waking me up.

"You talk too much, Wuthering Heights, as I have told you so often before. It is your next worst fault, and you ought to try your best to break yourself of it. I—"

"Ah, indeed yes, gnädige Frau, it is the very truth you are speaking, none knows it better than I nor is sorrier. Jesus!

but it is a verdammtes defect, as in your goodness you have said, yourself, these fifty times, and—"

"Don't! I never use such language—and I don't like to hear it. It is dreadful. I know that it means nothing with you, and that it is common custom and came to you with your mother's milk; but it distresses me to hear it, and besides you are always putting it into *my* mouth, which—"

"Oh, bless your kind heart, gnädige Frau, you won't mind it in the least, after a little; it's only because it is strange and new to you now, that it isn't pleasant; but that will wear off in a little while, and then—oh, it's just one of those little trifling things that don't amount to a straw, you know—why, we all swear, the priest and everybody, and it's nothing, really nothing at all; but I will break myself of it, I will indeed, and this very moment will I begin, for I have lived here and there in my time, and seen things, and learned wisdom, and I know, better than a many another, that there is only one right time to begin a thing, and that is on the spot. Ah yes, by Gott, as your grace was saying only yesterday—"

"There—do be still! It is as much as a person's life is worth to make even the triflingest remark to you, it brings such a flood. And any moment your chatter may wake my husband, and he"—after a little pause, to gather courage for a deliberate mis-statement—"he can't abide it."

"I will be as the grave! I will, indeed, for sleep is to the tired, sleep is the medicine that heals the weary spirit. Heilige Mutter Gottes! before I—"

"Be *still!*"

"Zu befehl. If—"

"*Still!*"

After a little pause the Executive began a tactful and low-temperature lecture which had all the ear-marks of preparation about it. I know that easy, impromptu style, and how it is manufactured, for I have worked at that trade myself. I have forgotten to mention that Wuthering Heights has not always served in a subordinate position; she has been housekeeper in a rich family in Vienna for the past ten years; consequently the habit of bossing is still strong upon her, naturally enough.

"The cook and Charlotte complain that you interfere in their affairs. It is not right. It is not your place to do that."

"Oh, Joseph and Mary, Deuteronomy and all the saints! Think of that! Why, of course when the mistress is not in the house it is necessary that somebody—"

"No, it is not necessary at all. The cook says that the reason the coffee was cold yesterday morning was, that you removed it from the stove, and that when she put it back you removed it again."

"Ah, but what *would* one do, gnädige Frau? It was all boiling away."

"No matter, it was not your affair. And yesterday morning you would not let Madame Blank into the house, and told her no one was at home. My husband was at home. It was too bad—and she had come all the way from Vienna. Why did you do that?"

"Let her in?—I ask you would I let her in? and he hard at his work and not wishing to be disturbed, sunk in his labors up to his eyes and grinding out God knows what, for it is beyond me, though it has my sympathy, and none feels for him more than I do when he is in his lyings-in, that way—now *would* I let her in to break up his work in that idle way and she with no rational thing in the world to pester him about? now *could* I?"

"How do you know what she wanted?"

The shot struck in an unprotected place, and made silence for several seconds, for W.H. was not prepared for it and could not think of an answer right away. Then she recovered herself and said—

"Well—well, it was like this. Well, she—of course she could have had something proper and rational on her mind, but then I knew that if that was the case she would write, not come all the way out here from Vienna to—"

"Did you know she came from Vienna?"

I knew by the silence that another unfortified place had been hit. Then—

"Well, I—that is—well, she had that kind of a look which you have noticed upon a person when—when—"

"When what?"

"She—well, she *had* that kind of a look, anyway; for—"

"How did you know my husband did not want to be disturbed?"

"Know it? Oh, indeed, and well I knew it; for he was that busy that the sweat was leaking through the floor, and I said to the cook, said I—"

"He didn't do a stroke of work the whole day, but sat in the balcony smoking and reading." [In a private tone, touched with shame: "reading his own books—he is always doing it."] "You should have told him; he would have been very glad to see Madame Blank, and was disappointed when he found out what had happened. He said so, himself."

"Oh, indeed, yes, dear gnädige Frau, he would *say* it, that he would, but give your heart peace, he is always saying things which—why, I was saying to the butcher's wife no longer ago than day before yesterday—"

"*Ruhig!* and let me go on. You do twice as much of the talking as you allow me to do, and I can't have it. If—"

"It's Viennese, gnädige Frau. Custom, you see; that's just it. We all do it; it's Viennese."

"But I'm not Viennese. And I can't get reconciled to it. And your interruptions—why, it makes no difference: if I am planning with the cook, or commissioning a dienstman, or asking the postman about the trains, no matter, you break right in, uninvited, and take charge of the whole matter, and—"

"Ah, Jessus! it's just as I was saying, and how true was the word! It's Viennese—all over, Viennese. Custom, you see— all custom. Sorel Blgwrxczlzbzockowicz—she's the Princess Tzwzfzhopowic's maid—she says she always does so, and the Princess likes it, and—"

"But I am not the Princess, and I want things *my* way; can't you understand a simple thing like that? And there's another thing. Between the time that the three of us went to Vienna yesterday morning, and ten at night when we returned, you seem to have had your hands overfull. When the cook's old grandfather came to see her, what did you meddle, for?"

THE QUARREL IN THE STRONG-BOX

Upon a certain occasion a quarrel arose among the Money in the banker's strong-box, upon matters of right and privilege. It began between a Nickel and a Copper. In conversation the Nickel chanced to make a disparaging remark about the Copper, whereupon the latter spoke up with heat and said—

"I will have you to know that I am as good as you are."

"Since when?" retorted the Nickel, with scorn.

"Since the Declaration of Independence said 'all money is created free and equal.' What do you say to that?"

"I say it is nothing but a form of speech, and isn't true. You know quite well that in society I am more welcome than you are; that more deference is paid to me than to you, and that no one would grant that you are equal in rank to me."

"Rank!" scoffed the Copper. "In a republic there is no such thing as rank. It is ignored by the highest authority in the land—the Constitution."

"What of it? So is discrimination in the matter of color. But it is a dead letter, and you know it. You colored people belong in the kitchen, and we won't allow you in the parlor, let the Constitution say what it will. You affect to repudiate rank, yet you have a rank of your own. One can pick you out in a crowd in the dark by the mere smell of it."

"I beg your pardon," responded the Copper coldly; "that is not rank, but merely rankness, which is a quite different thing."

"Oh, call it by any name you prefer; to my mind the—"

"My friend," interrupted an emaciated half dollar in a sickly voice, "really I must beg of you to modify your shout a little; you should leave your beer-hall style behind you when you push yourself up toward the upper circles of society."

"Upper circles be damned!" exploded the Nickel, with beer-house ruggedness of speech; "I want you to understand that I'm as good as you, you poor disreputable ostracised bummer, going around everywhere letting on to be a person of means—brazenly pretending to be worth fifty cents when you can't pay for six beers to save your life. I would like to know who will be putting on airs next. First it's this mulatto here whose social intercourse is restricted to the peanut stand and the poor-box, and now it is you!—you who have ceased to be Money, and have gone down, down, down, until now you are nothing but a Commodity, like potatoes and guano."

"It is true, I am temporarily in misfortune, yet I am nevertheless your superior in rank let the Declaration say what it will; and as I am in impaired health and the odor of stale beer is a damage to me, I shall be obliged if you will move a little further away and—"

"You also!" sniffed a Ten-Dollar Gold-Piece, with its handkerchief to its nose; "for from long usage as a tip you are foul with the noisome fragrance of greasy palms, and to a person of my rank and social condition nothing is more offensive than that."

"I am as good as you are, dear sir, and I will not move."

"Then I will."

"Not at my expense if you please," said a Hundred Dollar Bill, with asperity. "You are crowding me, and I will not have it. It passes my comprehension—the effrontery of this banker in subjecting me to the vulgar contact of all sorts of—"

"Now *you* are crowding *me!*" whimpered a Thousand Dollar Bond, "and I positively cannot have my snowy garments smirched by your—your—"

"Take that for your impudence!" cried the Hundred Dollar Bill, striking the Bond fairly in the face, and leaving a broad smirch of green ink there, "by the Declaration I am as good as you, and will prove it upon your body." And straightway the fighting was taken up by the metal moneys and became general; and soon the furious jingling and jangling frightened away a team of arriving burglars and brought the police.

And so it came to pass that the court, and not the disputants, solved the question in dispute. In delivering judgment his Honor said as follows.

"The contention that you are all created free and equal is correct.

"But both here in America and in foreign lands the meaning of that phrase is curiously misunderstood. It does not propose to set aside the law of Nature—which is, that her children are created *un*equal, and of necessity *must* be. They are unequal in strength, health, stature, weight, comeliness, complexion, intellect, and so on. The Constitution cannot alter that and has not tried to. It only makes all equal in one way: it gives each an equal right with his neighbor to exercise his talent, whatever it may be, thus making free to all, many roads to profit and honor which were once arbitrarily restricted to the few." He turned to a Copper and asked, "How much do you earn per year?"

"Five per cent, your Honor."

"Nickel, how much do you earn?"

"Five per cent."

"And you, Half Dollar?"

"Five per cent. That is, on what liars and slanderers are pleased to term my 'actual' value," snapped out the Depreci-ated, with a white flash of anger, at the same time turning his back to hide his tears, which were beginning to drip down over his "In God We Trust"—for he was one of that over-confident early mintage.

"What do you earn, Gold-Piece?"

"Five per cent."

"Hundred Dollar Bill?"

"Five per cent."

"Thousand Dollar Bond?"

"Five per cent."

"Very well. You perceive that you are all on a strictly dead level of equality; each gets the full market value of his talent, whether his talent is large or small; no advantage allowed any one of you on account of birth, station or quality. It is five per cent for all. If you were all Thousand Dollar Bonds you would all earn fifty dollars a year; if you were all Pennies, you would earn half a mill. If you were all Locomotives you could draw a train; if you were all Mice, you could draw a spool of thread. You are all equal in birth, you are all equal before the law, you are all born to 5 per cent. But the equality begins and ends there." He cast a withering glance at the Half Dollar, and concluded thus: "I am sorry to say that we have among us a few would-be Aristocrats, who claim a fictitious superiority not recognizable by the Constitution of our democracy. It profits them nothing. They get but their 5 per cent; and they get it on what they *are*, not on what they pretend to be."

Observation. This fable teaches us that the character of the Equality established by our laws is commonly misunderstood on both sides of the water; and not oftener by the ignorant than by the ostensibly wise.

HAPPY MEMORIES OF THE
DENTAL CHAIR

Are all dentists active talkers? And have they come by this gift by inheritance? The barber was the first dentist; he had been pulling teeth for thousands of years before the earliest dental specialist made his appearance and became his professional child and heir; for thousands of years he had been *the* talker of talkers, and when his heir inherited and carried off the pattern of his barber-chair for use in the new field, doubtless he inherited along with it the barber's facility of speech, the gradually and patiently perfected marvel of those ages of faithful and pains-taking practice.

But these are deep questions of theology, philology, mathematics; with them we have nothing to do. We will come to the point. I was not able to remember that I had ever sat in a dentist's chair; I was not able to remember that I had ever had a pain in any tooth. And so it was a cold awakening to me when a dentist who had caught a fleeting glimpse of my interior when I was laughing at something which spread me wider open than usual, told me I ought to go to Dr. Riggs and get my teeth attended to. He said I had a certain disease of the teeth which had a scientific name but was sometimes called "Riggs's disease" because Dr. Riggs had invented a method of treating it which cured it in some instances and arrested its progress and rendered it harmless in all; whereas it had formerly refused to succumb to dental science. Having got a vicious looking gouging-iron out of his pocket to fondle, his gift of talk came to him at once, just the same as if he had been behind his chair with a waiting subject paling under him, and proceeded with his flow. He said that most people had Riggs's disease, especially people whose teeth appeared to be perfectly sound and flawless; said one did not often find it with bad teeth; said it was heritable—where it existed in the parents, it would usually be found in the children. He said it was in the nature of blood poisoning; a secretion decayed the bone-surface of the roots of the teeth, then the gums retreated from these surfaces, pus was engendered in the gums, the teeth began to loosen, and the man's general health was injured. He said that Dr. Riggs's method was to dig up under the gums with his instruments and carve and scrape all the dead bone away, down to the living bone; then the gums would return to their place, attach themselves to the living bone, and become healthy again. Then he went on to say that talk was generally wasted on a Riggs disease victim; there being no pain, they didn't mind the disease, and they did mind the desperate operation required to check the malady. By way of example, he instanced the case of a young woman who came to him to have her teeth examined. They were beautifully white and regular, and perfectly sound, and he told her so; but he also told her that the whole thirty-two were in danger, because Riggs's disease was at their roots. She was a teacher, and had a salary of seven or eight hundred dollars; but she refused to pay "any such price;" she hadn't any pain, and didn't choose to import any; she wouldn't take all that proposed thirty-two batches of agony as a gift, let alone go into the market and buy it. When the dentist had got this far, his gouging-iron slipped out of his hand, and this broke his connection and gave me a chance to get on first base with a question: which was, why he didn't propose to operate upon my Riggs disease himself. He said he doubted if any dentist could do the work quite as well as Riggs himself.

Dr. Riggs lives in my own town; so, when I reached home, I went to him. He was gray and venerable, and humane of aspect; but he had the calm, possessed, surgical look of a man who could endure pain in another person. I got in the chair and looked about me, noting the cuspidor at my left elbow, the convenient glass of water; the table at my right covered with long steel bodkins laid out in rows on a white napkin; then laid my head back in the rest, feeling pale and nervous, for this thing was all new to me; new and hellish, if I may use such a word without offense. The doctor bent over me, I spread my mouth, and he put a mirror the size of a nickel into it, and inspected it all around. And began to talk. Not swiftly, not excitedly; but evenly, smoothly, tranquilly. He said I must have smoked considerable tobacco in my time. I responded, as well as the mirror would let me—"tons." He said it was the best of preservatives for the teeth; and went on tapping around in there with the mirror and examining, while I made mental note of his remark for use against the anti-tobacco incendiaries.

Presently he laid the mirror aside, raked among his bodkins, selected one, gave it a pass or two over an "Arkansas stone," laid a rag over my chin, placed a couple of fingers where I could have closed on them, and approached my mouth with the bodkin, which he held in the grip of his other hand. I began to shrink into myself and curl together, in a cold nightmare of expectancy. There was a strength-exhausting pause; then the doctor eased up his attitude and began to tell me some particulars concerning the Riggs disease. He said, among other things, that he had known it to so affect a victim's health as to prostrate him and keep him bed-ridden and helpless during long intervals, the physicians doctoring his stomach, not suspecting that the chief trouble was in the teeth, and so failing to afford relief. He instanced the case of a lady who had lain thus for a long time, under the hands of the most noted physicians of New York, until she was so wasted away that she could be gathered up and carried in one's arms like a child. When the case came to him, at last, he stopped the medicines, went to work with his dental instruments, and she was presently sound and well.

Then he put his tool into my mouth, rooted it up under a gum and began to carve. He seemed to fetch away chips of bone the size of my hand. In truth, what he removed could hardly have been seen without a microscope, I suppose—but my imagination is a microscope. If I had been honest enough to speak my mind, I would have said "Ow!" to every dig, and shouted it; but I was ashamed to do that, and so only said "Um," in a low voice, and kept back the exclamation point. The doctor worked fast, and with a hand that was as sure as it was vigorous, though along at first I was all the time expecting the instrument would slip and carry away all my Riggs disease at one rake.

The doctor talked along entertainingly, and I responded "Um" when my turn came—which was when I was hurt or thought I was. I was hurt a little, of course, but I think the main discomfort about the operation was not the pain but the disagreeable sense of having my bone cut into; and then, too, your teeth are so near your ears, that the work sounds like digging gravel and shoveling coal. I could go through those two days of bone-scraping now without minding it much; but I was inexperienced, then, and my imagination exaggerated the pain out of all reason.

At the end of an hour, something was said about chloroform. I knew I did not need it myself, but I believed my imagination did; so I accepted the bottle, and after that I held it always in my hand, and put it to my nose whenever my imagination got too brisk. The chloroform created a radical change; it made everything comfortable and pleasant. The pains were about as sharp as they had been before, but they rather seemed to be impersonal pains; pains that belonged to the community in general, including me, but not me particularly, not me any more than the others. So I did not care for them any longer; I do not care for a pain unless I can have it all to myself. The doctor's voice seemed removed to a little distance and somewhat subdued, or muffled; but his work seemed more aggressive and vigorous than ever (as perhaps it was), and nearer by, too.

The chloroform introduced the subject of anaesthetics, and the doctor told me about the first painless operation that was ever performed in this world; and his story had a most vivid interest, for the reason that he was the operator himself. We have been so accustomed, all our lives, to hearing about painless surgical operations, that I was as well prepared to be confronted by Columbus himself as to find myself in the living presence of the man who was midwife at the birth of the most merciful, the most beneficent of all the gracious host of the children of Science, the application of anaesthetics to the banishment of human agony. Yet it was true. The world had gone on enduring torture a thousand ages, and then science brought a miracle for its relief worth more than all the miracles that had ever preceded it; and had placed it, as her generous custom is, within the reach of every sufferer, instead of restricting it to a pious half dozen, after the old way. And this prodigious event itself had happened so long ago that it seemed part and parcel with the dim and dreamy antiquities; and yet it was certainly true that here was a man who was there at the time, and saw the thing done; was there, and himself inaugurated an event of such vast influence, magnitude, importance, that one may truly say it hardly has its equal in human history.

It was my ignorance that had made the event so old. It had happened in 1835. The doctor was a young dentist, then, and had just set up his shingle with young Wells. They visited a traveling laughing-gas exhibition one winter night, and were consumed with laughter over the grotesque performances of some of the Hartford youth while under the happy dominion of the gas. Presently one of them, a young chap named Cooley, went sprawling over a chair or a table, and reached the stage with a crash, but immediately jumped up and plunged into the fun again with no diminution of spirit.

I was in the chair a good part of two days—nine hours the first day and five the next—and then came out of it with my thirty-two teeth as polished and ship-shape and raw as if they had been taken out of the sockets and filed. It was a good job, and quickly and skilfully done; but if I opened my mouth and drew in a cold breath it woke up my attention like pouring ice water down my back. I could not touch anything to my teeth for several days, they were so supernaturally sensitive. But after that they became as tough as iron, and a thorough comfort. If by some blessed accident my conscience could catch the Riggs disease, I know what I would do with it.

My teeth had lasted more than twenty years longer than people's teeth usually last, but they had begun to develop specks of decay here and there, and the doctor said that these places ought to be gouged out and filled; but I had had enough holiday for the present, and said I would chance them five or six years longer. Friends told me that they might all get to decaying in that time; but I doubted it and went my own way.

That was my first experience in dentistry. Physically, I mean, though not pecuniarily. I had paid plenty of dental bills, but had not made one before. When my six-year limit was up, I went to the doctor again, and he found, sure enough, that my harvest was fine and large and ripe for the sickle. I had to put the thing off, for a while, as I was just leaving for the summer; but as soon as I got a chance I hunted up a dentist.

DR. VAN DYKE AS A MAN
AND AS A FISHERMAN

Last night I read in the *Atlantic* a passage from one of Rev. Dr. Van Dyke's books, and I cut it out, with a vaguely defined notion that I might need it sometime or other, by and by. I like Van Dyke, and I greatly admire his literary style—this notwithstanding the drawback that a good deal of his literary product is of a religious sort. He is about 35 years old, he is a Presbyterian, he is a clergyman, he is a member of the faculty of Princeton University. Still, I like him and admire him, notwithstanding.

This forenoon I was lounging along Fifth avenue, and I stopped opposite the Roman Catholic cathedral to contemplate the crowd massed in front of the edifice. It is a grand Catholic day—a grand Catholic week, in fact. There's a cardinal here with a message from the Pope, there are sixty bishops on hand, and there is to be great doings. A hand touched my shoulder—it was Van Dyke's! We hadn't met for a year. He nodded toward the multitude, and said:

"What do you think of it? Doesn't it warm your heart? They are ignorant and poor, but they have faith, they have belief, and it uplifts them, it makes them free. They have feelings, they have views, convictions, and they live under a flag where they have no master, and where they have the right and the privilege of doing their own thinking, and of acting according to their preference, unmolested. What do you think of it?"

"I think you have misinterpreted some of the details. You think that these people think. You know better. They don't think; they get all their ostensible thinkings at second hand; they get their feelings at second hand; they get their faith, their beliefs, their convictions at second hand. They are in no sense free. They are like you and me and like all the rest of the human race—slaves. Slaves of custom, slaves of circumstance, environment, association. This crowd is the human race in little. It is no trouble to love the human race, and we do love it, for it is a child, and one can't help loving a child; but the minute we set out to *admire* the race we do as you have done— select and admire qualities which it doesn't possess."

And so on and so on; we argued and argued, and arrived

where we began: he clung to his reverence for the race as the grandest of the Creator's inventions, and I clung to my conviction that it was not an invention to be really proud of. We had settled nothing. We were quiet for a while, and loafed peaceably along down the street. Then he took up the matter again. He reminded me that there were certain undeniably fine and beautiful qualities in our human nature. To wit, that we are brave, and hate cowardly acts; that we are loyal and true, and hate treachery and deceit; that we are just and fair and honorable, and hate injustice and unfairness; that we pity the weak, and protect them from wrong and harm; that we magnanimously stand between the oppressor and the oppressed, and between the man of cruel disposition and his friendless victim.

I asked him if he was acquainted with this person.

He said he was—hundreds of him; that, broadly speaking, he had been describing a Christian; that a Christian, at his best, was just such a person as he had been portraying. I said—

"I know a very good Christian who cannot fill this bill—nor any detail of it, in fact."

"I must take that as a jest," he said, lightly.

"No, not a jest."

"Then as at least an extravagance, an exaggeration?"

"No, as fact, simple fact. And I am not speaking of a commonplace Christian, but of a high-class one; one whose Christian record is without spot; one who can take rank, unchallenged, with the very best. I have not known a better; and I love him and admire him."

"Come—you love and admire him, and yet he cannot fill any single detail of that beautiful character which I have portrayed?"

"Not a single one. Let me describe one of his performances. He conceived the idea of getting some pleasure out of deceiving, beguiling, swindling, pursuing, frightening, capturing, torturing, mutilating and murdering a child—"

"Im-possible!"

"A child that had never done him any harm; a child that was gratefully enjoying its innocent life and liberty, and not suspecting that any one would want to take them away from it—for any reason, least of all for the mere pleasure of it. And so—"

"You are describing a Christian? There is no such Christian. You are describing a madman."

"No, a Christian—as good a one as lives. He sought out the child where it was playing, and offered it some dainties—offered them cunningly, persuasively, treacherously, cowardly, and the child, mistaking him for one who meant it a kindness, thankfully swallowed the dainties—then fled away in pain and terror, for the gift was poisoned. The man was full of joy at the success of his ingenious fraud, and chased the frightened child from one refuge to another for an hour, in a delirium of delight, and finally caught it and killed it; and by his eloquent enthusiasms one could see that he was as proud of his exploit as ever brave knight was, of deceiving, beguiling, betraying and destroying a cruel and wicked and pestilent giant thirty feet high. There—do you see? Is there any resemblance between this Christian and yours? This one was not brave, but the reverse of it; he was not fair and honorable, he was a deceiver, a beguiler, a swindler, he took advantage of ignorant trustfulness and betrayed it; he had no pity for distress and fright and pain, but took a frenzied delight in causing them, and watching the effects. He was no protector of threatened liberty and menaced life, but took them both. And did it for fun. Merely for fun. But you seem to doubt me. Here is his own account of it; read it yourself; I clipped it out of the *Atlantic* last night. For 'fish' in the text, read 'child.' There is no other difference. It is a Christian in both cases, and in both cases the human race is exposed for what it is—a self-admiring humbug."

As a point of departure, listen to a quotation from Dr. Henry van Dyke:—

"Chrr! sings the reel. The line tightens. The little rod firmly gripped in my hands bends into a bow of beauty, and a hundred feet behind us a splendid silver salmon leaps into the air. 'What is it?' cries the gypsy, 'a fish?' It is a fish, indeed, a noble ouananiche, and well hooked. Now if the gulls were here who grab little fish suddenly and never give them a chance; and if the mealy-mouthed sentimentalists were here, who like their fish slowly strangled to death in nets, they should see a fairer method of angling.

"The weight of the fish is twenty times that of the rod against which he matches himself. The tiny hook is caught painlessly in the gristle of his jaws. The line is long and light. He has the whole lake to play in, and he uses almost all of it, running, leaping, sounding the deep water, turning suddenly to get a slack line. The gypsy, tremendously excited, manages the boat with perfect skill, rowing this way and that way, advancing or backing water to meet the tactics of the fish, and doing the most important part of the work.

"After half an hour the ouananiche begins to grow tired and can be reeled in near to the boat. We can

see him distinctly as he gleams in the dark water. It is time to think of landing him. Then we remember with a flash of despair that we have no landing-net! To lift him from the water by this line would break it in an instant. There is not a foot of the rocky shore smooth enough to beach him on. Our caps are far too small to use as a net for such a fish. What to do? We must row around with him gently and quietly for another ten minutes, until he is quite weary and tame. Now let me draw him softly toward the boat, slip my fingers under his gills to give a firm hold, and lift him quickly over the gunwale before he can gasp or kick. A tap on the head with the empty rod-case,—here he is,—the prettiest land-locked salmon that I ever saw, plump, round, perfectly shaped and colored, and just six and a half pounds in weight, the record fish of Jordan Pond."

We had a very good time together for an hour. And didn't agree about anything. But it was for this reason that we had a good time, disagreement being the salt of a talk. Van Dyke is a good instance of a certain fact: that outside of a man's own specialty, his thinkings are poor and slipshod, and his conclusions not valuable. Van Dyke's specialty is English literature; he has studied it with deep and eager interest, and with an alert and splendid intelligence. With the result that the sound-ness of his judgments upon it is not to be lightly challenged by anybody. But he doesn't know any more about the human being than the President does, or the Pope, or the philoso-phers, or the cat. I wanted to give him a copy of my privately printed, unsigned, unacknowledged and unpublished gospel, "What is Man?" for his enlightenment, but thought better of it. He wouldn't understand it.

ON POSTAGE RATES ON
AUTHORS' MANUSCRIPT

Reader, suppose you were an idiot. And suppose you were a member of Congress. But I repeat myself. Simply suppose you were a member of Congress. And suppose you started-up what you believed to be your faculties, and worked out the draft of a law to cover the needs of some industry or other which you did not know anything about. What would you do with that draft—submit it to somebody who did know something about it, and get instruction and advice? Yes?

It is natural to think that; but the member of Congress proceeds differently. He drafts that law to cover a matter which he knows nothing about; he straightway submits it to the rest of the National Asylum, who are similarly ignorant concerning the thing; they amend-out any accidental clearnesses or coherences which may have escaped his notice; then they pass it, and it presently goes into effect. It goes into effect, and of course it begins to confuse and hamper interested parties, because they do not understand it. But this has been foreseen, and has also been provided for—in a most curious way. Each public department at Washington keeps a minor asylum of salaried inmates whose business it is to invent a meaning for laws that have no meaning; and to detect meanings, where any exist, and distort and confuse them. This process is called "interpreting." And sublime and awe-inspiring is this art!

Consider one specimen, then we will move along to the main purpose of this article: The law forbids the importation of pirated American books—intends to, at any rate; it certainly thought it forbade such importations. Well, Postmaster General Jewell entered into a convention with the Postmaster General of Canada which permits pirated American books to be sent into this country in the United States mail! and more than that, the United States government actually levies and pockets a duty on this contraband stuff! There, you see, is a law whose intent—though poorly and pitifully supported, as to penalties—was in the interest of the citizen; but the interpretation is wholly in the interest of the foreigner, and that foreigner a thief. And who gets any real benefit out of it? The thief makes a hundred dollars, the United States get a hundred dollars, and the American author loses a thousand, possibly ten thousand. How long will the thing remain in this way? Necessarily until a Congressman who is not a fool shall re-draft the copyright law; and have at his back a sufficiency of Congressmen also not fools, to pass it; and by luck hit upon an interval when they chance to be out of idiots in the interpretation-retreat of the Departments, and consequently no immediate way available to misconstrue its language and defeat its intent. Six hundred years, think? Or would you be frank, and say six hundred thousand?

And now let us stop prefacing, and pass to the real subject of this article. In old times, postage was very high: ten, fifteen, twenty-five cents on a single letter. Take fifteen hundred pages of manuscript, for a book, and apply those rates to the package, and what is the result? We have a couple of historical illustrations. An American girl shipped her manuscript book across the ocean to get Sir Walter Scott's "candid opinion" upon it—that is to say, a fulsome puff. She discreetly left him to pay the postage, which he did—twenty-five dollars! But, being afraid that that copy might chance to get lost, she shipped him a duplicate by the next vessel. He paid the postage again—twenty-five dollars. In this case, Sir Walter paid; but if the girl had sent her book to a publisher, she would have been careful not to invite his prejudice—she would have prepaid. When the publisher declined it and sent it back—a thing which publishers usually did then, and usually do yet—he would be sure to leave her to pay again. So she would be out of pocket the probable value of the book and forty-nine dollars besides. The same with the friends who had been incautious enough to lend her the money. Would she stop there? No. We never do. She would go on shipping that MS. to publisher after publisher, until she had tried the whole thirteen then existing in this country—if her friends continued to believe in the immortal merit of the book; and they always do. Six hundred and fifty dollars gone for postage! No, let us call it six hundred and twenty-five, and consider, for the sake of argument, that the thirteenth publisher is a dare-devil, and accepts the book. He reads the rough proof, but sends a "revise" containing scattering markings, to her. The markings turn it into constructive manuscript, and so she has to pay letter postage on it—say a dollar a batch, twenty-five batches, in all. She corrects the revise, returns it with markings of her own—and pays another twenty-five on it. Now the sum total has really reached six hundred and fifty dollars for the item of postage on the book. When it is published will she get the money back? In most cases, no.

Here was a very heavy burden laid upon a few individuals,

and they of the recognized pauper class. In those days, forty-six books were accepted and published, per year, in the United States, and some fraction under fifteen hundred thousand rejected and returned. Please figure on that; I have lost my pencil. But any way it was somewhere along about seventy-five or eighty million dollars a year for book-postage, you see.

The government finally took hold of the thing and passed a law which afforded an immense relief. It said that "Authors' Manuscripts" should pass through the mails at the rate of a half cent per ounce—and I think it was still cheaper than that, at first. But even at that rate you could send a book manu-script clear across the country for half a dollar or a dollar. The law also allowed proof-sheets to come under the head of "Authors' MS."

There was high rejoicing among the literary tribe. Such a mighty impulse was given to literature that—but, I must not venture to reveal how many billions of books were offered and rejected during the next few years, lest I be disbelieved. All went swimmingly for a time. Then the Department-idiot went to interpreting the law; possibly, also, the Asylum fell to amending it—as to that, I do not know. At first, everything designed for publication was Authors' MS. Except, I believe, newspaper correspondence. I remember trying, a long time ago, to send a daily newspaper letter from San Francisco as

Authors' MS., and not succeeding. The lopping and barring-off began pretty early, and proceeded swiftly. Presently, one could send nothing but book and magazine MS., and proofs and revises. By and by magazine MS was shut off; and in 1871 I was refused permission to send a "Galaxy" article for other than letter postage, but was allowed to receive and return proof-sheets of it at the Authors' MS. rate!

But by that time, and even earlier, we had ceased to need the U.S. mail and its fickle and fluctuating charity, for the express companies had got into full swing, and their service was as cheap as the government's, and rather prompter and surer. So the custom of sending MS. books by mail soon died; and inasmuch as nothing remained privileged except proof-sheets, the law presently became a dead and useless cumberer of the statute books.

Eleven years winged their changeful flight—as the novels say. Eleven years winged their changeful flight, and last week came at last. I had been expressing book MS to Boston, a couple of chapters at a time, all summer, from a farm out in interior New York. One day I enveloped one of these thin batches; and just then I happened to think that twenty-five cents for it was bad economy; so I stuck a two-cent stamp on it, marked it "Authors' MS.," and sent it down by a friend. Whereupon ensued a conversation by telephone:

"Postoffice authorities say it must be open at both ends."

"Very well, open it at both ends."

Silence for ten minutes. Then—

"Authorities find no *proof-sheets* with it. Can't send it."

"What do they want with proof-sheets?"

"Law extends Author's privilege to book manuscript *only when accompanied by proof-sheets!*"

I sat down and waited for this piece of colossal idiocy to sink home and settle securely to its right place among my bric-a-brac collection of unpurchasable mental curiosities; then I said—

"How in the world am I to furnish a proof-sheet of *manuscript which has never been printed?*"

"I don't know; but that is what the Post Office Department of the United States requires."

"The Post Office Department of the United States is an Ass."

"Second the motion. But the law—or at least the official interpretation of it—is as I have said."

"Please borrow the book for me. I wish to see the inspired words with my own eyes."

Here they are. United States Official Postal Guide, for January, 1882. "Ruling," or interpretation No. 34, page 642:

"Book manuscript, manuscript for magazines, periodicals,

newspapers, and music manuscript, are now subject to full letter rates of postage, *except they be accompanied by* PROOF-SHEETS, *or corrected proof-sheets,* OF SUCH MANUSCRIPT, etc., etc."

There it is—read it for yourself. If that isn't the very dregs of human imbecility and ignorance, where shall you go to find it? Is there another idiot asylum outside the Post Office Department of the United States that can fellow that?

Look at it all around—inspect it in detail—for it is the gem-stupidity of all the ages. You see, they have admitted newspaper MS to the privilege, now; and have added music; and have restored the magazine and the periodical to their early place with book MS.—and by a simple turn of the wrist, and the most miraculous piece of leatherheadedness the world ever saw, the interpreter-idiot has shut every one of them out and made the law an absolute and hopeless nullity!

You think that if *you* were a law-builder or a salaried law-tinker, and didn't know anything about a matter which came officially before you, you would go and get advice and information from somebody who did know something about it, before you meddled with it. But I whisper in your ear, now, as I did in the outset, and say to you that those laborious and well-meaning, and complacent, but groping, and shell-headed and inadequate Washington tumble-bugs have not that useful habit.

THE MISSIONARY IN
WORLD-POLITICS

To the Editor of the Times.

SIR: I think you will grant that the source of religion and of patriotism is one and the same—the heart, not the head. It seems established by ages of history that none but the weakest and most valueless men can be persuaded to desert their flag or their religion. We regard as a base creature the man who deserts his flag and turns against his country, either when his country is in the right or when she is in the wrong. We hold in detestation the person who tries to beguile him to do it. We say loyalty is not matter of argument but of feeling—its seat is in the heart, not the brain. I do not know why we respect missionaries. Perhaps it is because they have not intruded here from Turkey or China or Polynesia to break our hearts by sapping away our children's faith and winning them to the worship of alien gods. We have lacked the opportunity to find out how a parent feels to see his child deriding and blaspheming the religion of its ancestors. We have lacked the opportunity of hearing a foreign missionary who has been forced upon us against our will lauding his own saints and gods and saying harsh things about ours. If, some time or other, we shall have these experiences, it will probably go hard with the missionary.

History teaches us that there is no capable missionary except fire and sword or the command of a king whose subjects have no voice in the government. Christianity, like Mohammedanism, has made its conquests by force, not persuasion. The Christendom of to-day is the result, solely, of the sword in some cases, and of royal mandate in the others. Since these two missionaries retired from the field the industry has stood still. Persuasion has accomplished nothing. Nothing, for the reason that for every convert it has made, more than a thousand pagans have been born to fill up his place. If the missionary trade had been a commercial enterprise, its sane and practical board of directors would have seen, two centuries ago, that there was no profit in it and no profit possible to it on this side of eternity, and they would have gone into liquidation, paid ha'pence in the pound, and taken in their sign;

reporting to the stockholders that "the balance of trade being 1,000 to 1 against us we have considered it wise to retire from the enterprise and apply our energies to something worth while." But mission-propagators are apparently not open to (business) logic. They have paid out millions upon millions of pounds to add an almost invisible Christian fringe around the globe's massed heathen billions; they are aware that the body of the fabric increases in bulk a thousand times faster than the fringe; they know that a convert is by far the most expensive bric-a-brac in commerce; they know that if he is a grown-up convert he is as a rule a poor thing and always a traitor, and was not worth harvesting at any figure. And yet they are quite well satisfied with the triumphs they are achieving. That is the name they usually call it by.

Still, if it amuses the missionary and his backer, should the man in the street object? Is it any of his affair? Is he in any way affected by it? Does it do him any harm? It is a question worth considering. Let him put himself in the pagan's place, and examine some of the facts by that light. Wherever the missionary goes he not only proclaims that his religion is the best one, but that it is a true one while his hearer's religion is a false one; that the pagan's gods are inventions of the imagination; that the things and the names which are sacred to him are not worthy of his reverence; that his fathers are all in hell, and the dead darlings of his nursery also, because the word which saves had not been brought to them; that he must now desert his ancient religion and give allegiance to the new one or he will follow his fathers and his lost darlings to the eternal fires. The missionary must teach these things, for he has his orders; and there is no trick of language, there is no art of words, that can so phrase them that they are not an insult. In Fiji the old pagan said, "And all I loved are in hell? I am not a dog; I will follow them." That a missionary ever survives his first exhibition of his samples shows that there is something very fine and patient and noble about the pagan. It seems a pity to ever missionary it out of him. When a French nun in Hong Kong proposed to send to France for money wherewith to establish an asylum for fatherless little foundlings where they might be fatted up physically and spiritually, the authorities said, "How kind of you to think of us—are you out of foundlings at home?" The missionary has no wish to be an insulter, but how is he to help it? All his propositions are insults, word them as he may. In an ignorant and bigoted Chinese village the mere sight of him is an insult—particularly when he is there by grace of foreign force. Two hundred years ago the Chinese hated him, ordered him away, and slaughtered him when he tarried. They have hated him ever since, and henceforth they will hate him more than ever.

And have they not reason for it? When a white man there kills a Chinaman is he dealt with more severely than he would be in Europe? No. When a missionary is killed by a Chinaman, are the Chinese blind to the difference in results? When an English missionary was lately killed there in a village, a British official visited the place and arranged the punishments himself—exacted them and secured them: a couple of beheadings; several sentences to prison, one of them for ten years; a heavy fine; and the village had to put up a monument and also build a Christian chapel to remember the missionary by. If we added fines and monuments and memorial churches to murder-penalties at home—but we don't; and we do not add them in China except when it is a missionary that is killed. And then they are insults, and they rankle in the Chinese breast, and bring us no advantage, moral, political, or commercial. But they move the Chinaman to ponder dubiously upon the meek and forgiving religion and its pet child the gilded and feathered "civilization" which the Christian Governments are so anxious to confer upon him.

Two years ago the Chinese killed a German missionary. The German Government sent in its bill promptly, and it was paid: £40,000 cash; a new Christian church; and a "lease" of sea-bordered territory twelve miles deep. Would Germany have ventured to charge so much if the missionary had been killed in Russia or England? And does not this question rise in the Chinaman's mind and move him to anger? Would the charge have been made for any German but a missionary? If there had been no missionaries in China would there be any trouble there to-day? I believe not. Commercial foreigners get along well enough with the Chinese. But the missionary has always been a danger, and has made trouble more than once. He was Germany's happy opportunity: when he is not making trouble himself we perceive that he can be a calamitous pretext for it. He must be held responsible for the present condition of things in China and for the massacre of the Ministers. We are told that Germany's act was the thing which finally broke down the Chinaman's patience and started the present upheaval. If that missionary had only been a German sailor he would have been settled for on terms which would have added no affronting memorial churches to China and bred no bad blood.

He has surpassed all his former mischiefs this time. He has loaded vast China onto the Concert of Christian Birds of Prey; and they were glad, smelling carrion; but they have lit and are astonished, finding the carcase alive. And it may remain alive—Europe cannot tell, yet. If the Concert cannot agree, they cannot appoint a Generalissimo; without a Generalissimo they can have plenty of scattered picnics, but no general holiday excursion in China. And it is not unlikely that the picnic parties will fall out among themselves. That the Concert can agree and stay so, no one believes, not even the office-cat. The China war may turn out a European war, and China go free and save herself alive. Then, when the world settles down again, let us hope that the missionary's industries will be restricted to his native land for all time to come. Is the man in the street concerned? I think he is. The time is grave. The future is blacker than has been any future which any person now living has tried to peer into.

X

THE UNDERTAKER'S TALE

We did not drop suddenly upon the subject, but wandered into it in a natural way—I and my pleasant new acquaintance. He said it "was about this way"—and began:

Toward nightfall on the 14th of January, 18—, I trudged into the poor little village of Hydesburg. I had walked far, that day; at least it seemed far for a half-starved boy of fifteen to have come. I had lain in a barn the night before, and been discovered and roughly driven away early in the morning. I had begged for food and shelter at three farm houses during the day, but had been refused. At the last place the children set the dogs on me and I was glad to get away with some loss of flesh and a part of my rags. I was very hungry, now, and very tired. The wounds

made by the dogs were stiff and painful. I had been an outcast
for a month and had fared harshly all the time. I was hopeless,
now, and afraid to supplicate at any door.

The darkness drew on, the outlines of the village houses
grew vague, the lights began to twinkle in the windows. The
wind swept the street in furious gusts, driving a storm of
snow and sleet before it. I stopped in front of a small house
and leaned on the low fence, for there was a pleasant picture,
for an outcast, visible through one of the windows. It was a
family at supper. There was a roaring wood fire burning on
the hearth; there was a cat curled up in a chair, asleep; there
were some books on a what-not, some pictures on the walls;
but mainly there was the smoking supper; a benevolent looking man of middle age sat at the foot of the table; a motherly
dame at its head, and a little boy and girl at one side. It was
like looking into paradise.

I never once thought of knocking at that door. I had had
enough of cuffs and curses. I no longer believed that there
were men in the world who would pity me or any other miserable creature.

It was very dark, now. A man who was running by behind
an umbrella, struck against me with such a shock that both of
us fell. He cursed me roundly as he gathered himself up, and
gave me a good-bye kick as he left. It caught me on one of my

dog-bites and made me cry out with the pain. Then he was lost in the darkness and the driving storm. But a sweet girlish voice said, "Poor thing, are you hurt?" and I saw a dim figure bending over me. I said—

"I only stopped just a minute. I was not meaning any harm, please. I am going away, now."

The girl said—

"Going away? Where? Do you live in the village?"

"No, please."

"Then where are you going, such a night as this?"

"I don't know."

"What! Haven't you any place to stay?"

"No."

"Nor any friends?"

"No."

"Yes you have!"

"Where?"

"There—in the house—my father's house. We are your friends. Come."

She helped me up, and tried to lead me toward the door, whereat I was very glad for a moment, but then straightway afraid again. So I said—

"Please let me go away, and I will not come any more. Honest, I will not."

But it was no use. The girl dragged me into the house, I expecting nothing else but to be hustled out again the next moment. But it was not so. The whole family gathered about me, took me to the fire, and more warmed me with their pitying words than the fire did.

I carried a full stomach to a good bed that night. And I worshiped those people, knowing no gods but these nor desiring any other.

II

When two weeks had gone by, from that time, my former life had dimmed to a dream. It seemed to me as if I had always been a part of this dear good loving family. I called Mr. Cadaver father and his wife mother. Jimmy and Mary and Grace were brother and sisters to me. Grace was the one that saved me. She was eighteen years old, and so fair and shapely, and so sweet and so unapproachably beautiful that it was heaven to me to look at her face and listen to her voice.

Business was prosperous, and we were all as blithe and happy as birds. I became useful in many ways and felt the gratification of knowing that I was earning the bread I ate. I learned to assist Grace in decorating the insides of the coffins with pleated cambrics or costlier stuffs, according to the requirements of the customers. We talked and sang by the hour while we made crosses of flowers or wreathed immortelles. Sometimes, as she wrought with her nimble needle upon a shroud, she would tell me the simple history of the person who was to wear it; for it was but a little village, and she knew all about everybody. All day long the music of her father's plane was heard in the back shop, and we lived in an atmosphere of deep peace and contentment. I learned to arrange the coffins in the front shop so as to get the best effects, gracing the neat rows with festoons of crape depending from immortelles fastened against the walls, with here and there a soft white shroud and in the intervals finely polished coffin plates that reflected the sunlight almost like mirrors. I took care of the horse, and was often allowed to drive the hearse. There was no rival in our business in the village. We had it all.

But by and by there came an evil day. I will tell about this. Gracie had a sweetheart whom she dearly loved and had promised to marry. This was a most excellent young man named Joseph Parker, who had commenced life in the humblest circumstances, but had risen by honest endeavor till he was now sexton to the village church, and grave digger. The graveyard was owned by several citizens, who presently wished to sell it. It was pleasantly located on a hill side and very desirable. Young Parker conceived the idea of buying it. It was a great chance, but the price was a vast one, being six hundred dollars, and he had no money. Mr. Cadaver loved Joseph, and he could not bear to see this opportunity lost; he looked from Grace's beseeching eyes to Joseph's and his heart was touched. He said—

"You shall have the graveyard, my children; take yourselves off, now, and be happy."

You should have seen Gracie throw her arms around his neck, and pat his cheek and cry for joy.

So Mr. Cadaver mortgaged his house for the six hundred dollars, borrowed the money of old Marlow the skinflint, and the beautiful graveyard was Joseph's. That was a happy night. We all sat around the fire, Joseph with Gracie's little hand in his, and all the talk was of how good and sweet was life. Joseph said—

"If we have a good season, I can pay off the debt in six months."

"That will be a pleasant thing," said the old man; "and I think the signs are in favor of a good season. It is a very changeable winter, with much wet and much cold."

"Yes," said Mrs. Cadaver, "it is just such a winter as the one before Jimmy was born. There was ever so much croup and pneumonia in the spring."

"I remember it," said Gracie. "There was ever so much sickness, and very few got well. I remember father's saying he had never seen business so brisk."

Mr. Cadaver drew a long sigh. He said:

"Those were great days—great days. They don't often come. However, it is not for us to complain; that would be ungrateful indeed."

Grace smiled sweetly and said—

"Dear old father, to hear him talk, one would think he was afraid somebody might think him capable of being ungrateful. Why father, adversity only brings out your gentleness and patience. Do you remember the time that not one person died in this village during twenty-eight days? Were you downcast? Did you show any bitterness? No—not one angry word escaped your lips. You hardly even betrayed annoyance."

Mr. Cadaver kissed her cheek lovingly and patted her on the head. He said—

"There—there's your punishment, little flatterer!"

He beamed on her with fatherly pride, and there was moisture in his eyes. Gracie turned her pretty mouth toward Joseph, and said—

"How can you see me so cruelly punished and not protect me?"

"Because you deserved it, poor child—you deserved double what you got—and there 'tis!"

He kissed the rosy lips, and got a pretty little love-box on his ear for his pains. Everybody laughed, and we all fell to joking and chaffing and had such a good time. By and by Mr. Cadaver took down the old family Bible, put on his spectacles and reverently read a chapter, and then prayed. We always had family worship, morning and evening.

But as I said before, trouble was to come. Business began to grow dull while the winter was still upon us. It steadily slackened. Presently it had so dwindled that there was no trade but in chronic consumptions, and it is hardly worth while to mention that there is never much doing in cases of that sort in little country villages. The joy in the faces of the family gradually gave way to anxious looks, and we had but little pleasant talk, evenings. Things only grew worse as time went on. The spring opened gloomily. We had day after day of brilliant sunshine, clamor of warbling birds, balmy, healing, vivifying atmosphere—there was everything to make us dismal, heartsick, hopeless. The spring dragged its disastrous length along and left a memorable record behind it—three months and a half with scarcely a demise.

We got ready for the summer trade. There came news that the cholera had appeared in the seaports, and for the first time in months we had an old-time evening of innocent gaiety in place of bowed heads and heavy sighs. The disease spread from village to village, till it reached within five miles of us—then it split apart and wandered far away on either side, leaving our town untouched!

"It is very hard," said Mr. Cadaver, and we saw the tears trickle through his fingers as he sat with his hands clasped over his face, rocking to and fro and softly moaning.

Once it had been our happiness on peaceful Sabbath afternoons, to stroll to Joseph's graveyard and count the new mounds and talk of the prospects. But this had long ceased. There were no new mounds any more; the turf had grown old upon all; there was no longer anything about the graveyard that could cheer our hearts, but much to sadden them.

There came a time, at last, when we all realized that imminent disaster was hovering over us. Nothing had been paid on the graveyard and the six hundred dollars would soon fall due. Old Marlow got to haunting the place with his evil eye. He would intrude in the most unexpected way and remind Mr. Cadaver to get ready to move out of the house if the money was not forthcoming on the appointed day.

How the days flew! Once Mr. Cadaver appealed to him for a little time.

"Time!" cried old Marlow. "What on!"

"My business, Mr. Marlow."

"Business! Tush! You have none. What are your assets? Come—show them up, man."

Mr. Cadaver showed him his list of coffins and other stock, and also a list of neighbors who were very low. These latter Mr. Marlow derided—laughed over the list brutally. Said he—

"You call these people assets? There ain't one in the lot but will outlast this generation!"

"But sir, the doctor said this morning that old Mrs. Hale and Mr. Samson—"

"Bother what the doctor said! Mrs. Hale has been dying for ten years, and old Samson for fifteen. Call such stock as that, *assets*! The idea!"

"I have heard that George Simpson had a very bad night last night, and there is every hope—I mean every prospect that he—"

"Drop your hopes of George Simpson, my friend. He sat up in bed this morning and ate a fricasseed chicken."

Mr. Cadaver murmured with a sigh, "This is indeed an unexpected blow." He tried once more to throw a favorable aspect upon some of his assets, but Marlow scouted every name and said there was neither man, woman nor child in the list but would get well. He finally said:

"Hark ye! You have neglected your business till ruin stares you in the face and it serves you right."

"I, sir? I cannot bury people if they will not die. Please have pity—think of my poor family—do not be hard with me, Mr. Marlow. I am sure my assets are lower than you think them to be, and if you would only give me a little time to realize on them—"

"Not another word!" cried Marlow. "You will pay the last cent day after tomorrow or out of this house you go!"

He banged the door and went.

III

That next day was a day never to be forgotten. All day long the family sat grouped together, saying little, now and then looking into each other's stony eyes, now and then clasping each other in a long embrace, and many were the smothered sobs that were heard, many the tears that fell.

I could not bear this sight long at a time. I flitted restlessly from house to house where we had hopes, but gained no comfort. One client was "better to-day;" another "about the same;" another had a "stronger pulse;" another had had "an easier night than usual." Always these dismal refrains. Whenever I entered our stricken home, I had to meet the mute inquiry of those pathetic eyes, but I never had to speak—my own looks conveyed my heavy tidings and the hopeless heads were bowed once more.

I was up all night, wandering about the village. The fatal day came, the sun rose and still I wandered from house to house—but not to inquire—I had no heart to do that any longer. I only took friends of mine to these houses, and told them to wait, and if they got any news, to bring it to me with all speed.

Two hours later there was a scene in our home. Old Marlow was there, gloating over his victims. He paced the floor banging upon it with his stick and talking like this:

"Come, the sooner you clear out of this, the better you'll suit me. A pack of paupers, that is what you are! Fine assets, truly! Coffins rotting away without sale, a graveyard that's become a grazing ground, a gang of convalescents that the lightning couldn't make marketable!"

So he raved on, enjoying himself. One after another my friends came softly to the door, whispered their tidings to me and glided away. I let the old man storm on. At last my poor old Cadaver rose feebly up, gathered his weeping wife to his side, and said—

"Go, my little children, and you, my poor daughter and my poor Joseph, go forth from the old home; it has no shelter, more, for our breaking hearts. Out into the bleak world we will go together, and together will we starve and die."

And so, with bended heads and streaming eyes, they moved slow and sadly toward the door. Marlow waved his hand and said—

"Farewell, a long farewell! My house is well rid—"

"Hold!" I shouted. "Stay where you are!"

Everybody stared with inquiring astonishment. Old Marlow grew red with rage.

"What means this?" he cried.

"It means this!" said I. "Samson is no more! old Mrs. Hale is at peace! Philip Martin has fallen with apoplexy! William Thompson is drowned! George Simpson has had a relapse and the rattle is in his throat! And hark ye, wretch, the cholera is at our very doors and in its most malignant form!"

With a wild joy Mr. Cadaver threw his arms around my neck and murmured—

"O, precious, precious tidings!—blest be the tongue that has uttered them!"

Joseph and Gracie embraced with tears of gratitude, and then astounded me by embracing me, too. In an instant misery was gone and tumultuous happiness had taken its place. I turned upon old Marlow and said—

"There, sir, is the door, be gone! You will be paid, never

fear. And if you should want to borrow any money," I said, with bitter sarcasm, "do not hesitate to say so, for we can procure all we want, with our present business prospects."

He went away raging, and we went gaily to work dusting stock and getting ready for the most lucrative day's work our little shop had ever known.

Little remains to be told. Our prosperity moved straight along without a halt. Everything seemed to conspire to help us. No village in all the region was so ravaged by the pestilence as was ours, the doctors were the first to go, and those who supplied their places passed through our hands and Joseph's without halt or delay. The graveyard grew in grace and beauty day by day till there was not a grass-patch visible in it, not a level spot to trouble the eye.

All in good time Joseph and Gracie were married, and there was a great and costly wedding. As if to make everything complete and leave nothing to be desired, the commerce of the wedding day paid the entire expense of the occasion, and Mr. Marlow himself headed the procession in a sixty-dollar casket.

MARK TWAIN

THE MUSIC BOX

It was in Geneva that I got my music box. Everybody orders a watch, in Geneva, and a music box. Neither of these things was a necessity to me, but I ordered both, because I did not like to seem eccentric. The watch is perfectly satisfactory, and I shall not part with it, but as soon as I shall have decided which of my enemies I hate most, and most wish to afflict, I am going to give him my music box. When I asked after the best music-box establishment, I was told to go to that of Monsieur Samuel Troll, *fils,* in the rue Bonivard. So I went there, and found a young Englishman on duty, to whom I stated my business. He had probably been bothered a good deal with tourists who came merely to sample his goods for curiosity's sake, without any intention of buying; for he ex-

hibited a most composed indifference concerning the matter
in hand. He was not rude—very far from it; indeed he was
endowed with an enviable stock of polite graces and affable
superiorities—he was indifferent to matters of commerce,
that was all; he was not indifferent to other things, such as the
weather, the war-news, the opera, and so on; in fact he showed
a cheery and vivacious interest in these. Consequently, while
we progressed well enough, socially, we did not get along very
fast, commercially. Whenever he started a music box to grinding a tune, he immediately began to hum that tune himself,
and tap the time on the table, nodding his head from side to
side in unison with the measure. He was at his best and happiest and gracefulest, then, and seemed born to accompany a
music box. It is true that while the humming was artistic, and
carefully and conscientiously done, and compelled one to observe and admire how intimately the performer knew the tune,
it was in some sense an obstruction since it allured one's attention away from the music-box's efforts, and even made him
forget that there was any music box around. It also had the
effect of making one suspect that a music box bought in these
circumstances might prove a disappointment when it reached
home—it might have but a poor and inadequate sound, since
of course it would have no hummer attached. It seemed to me
wisest to quietly persist in having box after box tried, in the

hope that in the end we might run across one with a hummer to it. But no, the hope was vain. We tried fifty boxes, but they were all the wretched old-fashioned tinkling kind, with here and there one freighted with a nerve-wrenching accumulation of aggravating devices—such as little bells, and gongs, and drums, and castanets, and wing-flopping, beak-stretching singing-birds—a most maddening and inhuman invention. Not even a hummer could make this sort endurable.

But at last I was reluctantly shown—in a back room, the holy of holies of the establishment,—a trunk-like box which was altogether satisfactory. It occupied that place in solitary state, and I was told it was of a sort not kept in stock, but only made to order. It had none of the customary deviltries in its composition, but simply produced the soft, long-drawn strains and richly blended chords of flutes and violins playing in concert. Moreover, it needed no hummer; the humming seemed to even mar and mutilate its gentle and tranquilizing music.

I ordered a box like that one—and it was my own fault that I never got it. I thought I had ten favorite tunes, but easily found I had only four. It took me eight months to furnish the other six. Meantime I suppose that that young man had forgotten what kind of a box I had ordered. At any rate when I at last opened the blessed thing in America, the first turn of the crank brought forth an agonizing jingle and squawk and clatter of bells, gongs, drums, and castanets, with never a solitary strain of flute or fiddle! It was like ordering a serenade of angels, and getting a shivaree in place of it. The biggest box, of this sort, in Mr. Troll's establishment, had loosened half of my teeth with one of its mildest efforts—now here was one full four times as big, gifted with eleven times the destructive power—a machine capable of producing almost instant death. With duties, freights, and so on, it had cost me six hundred and fifty dollars—a pure waste, for I could have got a guillotine for half the money.

I did not know what to do with it. It did not seem safe to have it about the house where innocent and unsuspecting persons might meddle with it and I be held for damages on the inquest; neither would it be right to ask any storage-house to take charge of it without explaining its dangerous nature; I could not keep a policeman to watch it, for I could not afford to pay for that policeman in case he came to grief; I would not trust it in the cellar, for there was a good deal of machinery about it which nobody understood, and there was no sure thing that it would not go off of its own accord, and of course I could not collect any insurance on the damage it would do the house, for a fire-risk does not cover destruction wrought by a music box; I thought of burying it, but the sexton did not like to handle it. There was really no way out of the scrape. One neighbor took it home, at last, and put some wires to it, and started in to use it for a burglar alarm; but the first time it went off, (it was doing the Anvil Chorus,) this man, instead of rising up and killing the burglars, went quaking to them and offered them all his wealth to kill the music box. But they fled.

She is on my hands yet. I am willing to trade her for an elephant, and give boot. Or, I will agree to fight her with an elephant, the victor to yield up his champion to the vanquished.

She is not the box I ordered. Mr. Troll says she is; but as I was present and he was not, perhaps I ought to know better than he. He frankly offers to take her back if I will ship her to Geneva, and says he will give me the other kind of box. That is creditable, and is all he could be expected to do; but as my life and limbs are valuable to me I am not going to try to pack that thing in these times when accident policies are so high.

The moral of this little tale is, when you order a music box in Geneva, furnish your tunes at once, then no mistake will be made, and you will get what you order. But if you delay as I did, Mr. Troll's young man's memory may become uncertain and cause a disappointment to be inflicted upon you. No intentional wrong will be done you, for it is an honorable and trustworthy house, but no matter, if you delay too much you may have the bitterness of seeing that the charming instrument you have so long been waiting for is not that enchanting instrument at all, but a Gatling gun in disguise.

THE GRAND PRIX

The Grand Prix is the great race of the year in France; so the knowing all tell me; and they also tell me that it is to the Parisian fashionable season what the benediction is to a church service—it ends it. After the Grand Prix is run, the fashionables who can afford to go away to the summer resorts do so, and the fashionables who cannot, pretend to do it.

Everybody goes to the great race. It is in the spacious Park, the Bois de Boulogne. All the cabs and carriages are secured beforehand for that day, and by two in the afternoon Paris is a silent wilderness of empty and unpeopled streets. Men, women and children who may not ride, walk; for the distance is only three or four miles, and after one has left the Arch of

Triumph a short way behind, the rest of his road lies through the cool and shady lanes of the great forest.

We went as guests of a friend, resident in Paris. We started at one o'clock in the afternoon, and found that wonderful avenue, the Champs Elysee already crowded from end to end with a rushing tornado of vehicles, about eight abreast. It was a dry, sunny summer's day, yet there was no dust. After we got out of the city and entered the forest, we found the main roads crowded in the same way. These roads were fringed on both sides with policemen. I think I never saw so many policemen in one day before. If a horse grew restive, three or four of them were at his head in a moment; if anything occurred to block the procession, they swarmed into the road and started the forward movement again; they were at hand, always, to *prevent* disturbances as well as to put a stop to them. Without this active vigilance the innumerable caravan would have been in constant confusion, and consequently would have been hours making its short journey; a section of it could not stop and the rest go on—no, the checking of one section dammed the whole prodigious stream of four solid miles of vehicles. Through the watchfulness of the police the stream was enabled to flow swiftly on, with hardly ever an interruption.

It was a marvelous journey. It was as if the world was emigrating.

We reached the race course. Vast detachments of vehicles broke away from the procession and drove into the ample enclosure, but we went on with the main body. We passed several gates and ticket offices, and stopped at the gate nearest to the grand stand. Then the brilliant sun was suddenly eclipsed and the rain poured down in flooding torrents. One would naturally say, What of that?—a summer shower is nothing. But in the present circumstances it was a good deal; for the French ladies dress as for a dinner or a state ball when they go to this great national race. Hardly any of the carriages had been closed, so suddenly had the shower come. I saw scores of open carriages whirl by, whose occupants sat with heads bowed to the drenching cataract, while their gorgeous plumage wilted down and clung to their bodies in tripy corrugations like the wrinkles in a washer-woman's hand. In a twinkling the hard smooth road had an inch depth of mud and water on it. Into this mess those armies of richly dressed ladies had to insert their slippered feet. One pretty girl of twenty or thereabouts, clothed in a shining splendor of costly raiment, looked ruefully out of her carriage, then disclosed a shapely foot and ancle, and pointed the same toward the step—and halted a moment to gather the necessary courage to proceed. The ancle was enclosed in a cream-tinted stocking of so thin a texture that the flesh showed through, and the small foot was sandaled in the

daintiest of silken cream-tinted slippers, propped on the tall-
est of tapering heels. She made up her mind, she accepted the
woeful necessity. She advanced that graceful extremity further
forth from the sheltering drapery and rested it upon the carriage step; she stood upright and gathered the drapery about
her person and out of harm's reach; then she stepped down
and the yellow mud and the stained water swelled up and
overflowed the gunwale of the delicate slipper, and I helped
her do the shuddering. She waded off with her escort, carrying the most of her clothes on her left arm, and looking like an
airy creation of sea-foam and snow which would have seemed
to float on the breeze if the tapering cream-tinted calves had
been out of sight.

Meantime, while I was enjoying all this scenery, our friend
was buying the four tickets. We left the carriage, now, and
were admitted; but the moment we were fairly past the ticket-
examiner and safe in the grounds, a man in plain clothes
halted us and asked in French to be allowed to see our tickets.
They were shown to him.

"How much did you pay for these?"

"Twenty francs apiece."

"Where did you buy them?"

"At the office just outside this gate."

"Let me have them, if you please. Wait here a moment."

He disappeared in the crowd with our property before any of us thought to inquire what he wanted with it and by what authority he interested himself in our affairs. We stood under the umbrellas and discussed this pirate in a pretty vicious way. We also discussed ourselves and our points of resemblance to other kinds of fools. But presently our host said,—

"Nobody was in fault but me. Perhaps the lesson is worth what it has cost. Wait here a moment and I will go out and buy some more tickets, and this time we will see if we can't take care of them."

I remained with the two ladies, and he started off; but at that moment we saw our pirate shouldering his way toward us through the crowd. He gave us two red tickets, two pale yellow ones, and a gold twenty-franc piece, and said,—

"Your road is this way, messieurs,—to the right. Ladies pay only half price."

Then he bowed politely and immediately turned on his heel and collared another party of green foreigners who were trying to get their ladies in on twenty-franc tickets when ten-franc ones would answer just as well. I have encountered many government officers in Christian lands, whose business it was to see that the sojourner did not swindle the government; but I had never even heard of a government before which appointed officers to keep a lookout and see that the sojourner did not swindle himself.

We moved on, among the trees and the grass plats, and found the grand stand. It was already packed with ladies; there were a thousand or more, and the long ranks rose tier above tier backward to the rear wall of the building. The costumes were so gay and so splendid that this mass of color was like a hillside bedded in flowers. The roof of the building was packed, also—with both sexes. There were several other grand stands like this one, and they were crowded, too. In front of them all, extended a wide fenced space which sloped from the stands to the race track, and this unsheltered ground was furnished with some thousands of splint-bottomed chairs, free to anybody who had a ticket.

After the first race the people deserted the roof of the stand, and we went up there and got front seats and kept them the rest of the day. We could look out over the vast green level, now, which was enclosed by the race-track. It was thronged with carriages, cabs and drags,—a multitudinous host, massed into a compact body—a body to be reckoned rather by acre than by count. The sky was cloudless by this time; therefore the vehicles were without covers, and there was nothing to hide the acres of brilliant costumes or mar the effect of the sun upon them.

The fence-line for nearly half a mile enclosed a deep belt of men, women and children—I don't know how deep—it was a matter of acres again. When your eye followed the flying horses around, you observed that that entire great field was walled with people. It was a wonderful thing to see. Yes, coming out it had seemed to me that the world was emigrating; the emigration was finished, the world was here assembled together.

It was all beautiful, too; wherever the ground was visible it was carpeted with green grass; the dense green woods surrounded us and shut us into our verdant plain; above the woods rose two or three dim spires and towers of Paris, and in the blue sky floated the gray bubble of a distant balloon, whose passengers probably saw in our assembled world only a something which resembled a pretty extensive gathering of black ants.

Every race was awaited with interest and observed with considerable eagerness—but both the interest and the eagerness were well bred and never boisterous. There was a change, though, when the event of the day approached—the grand twenty-thousand-dollar race. The hosts gathered silently, but steadily and continuously, everywhere. There had been many vacant seats on our roof before, but there were none, now. The world in the green plain had had fringed edges before, and outlying detachments of stragglers, but it was solid, now. Solid and still. There was something very impressive about the waiting hush of this mighty sea of life. Twelve clean-limbed, glossy racers filed out upon the track, bearing riders clothed in all shades of new and glittering satin. They scampered down the track over the first quarter to limber themselves up, then marched, single file, by the stand, at a walk, in the order of their numbers upon the bulletin, and took their places for the start, a quarter of a mile to our right. There was a still pause of some minutes, then a low inarticulate murmur all about us, and we knew they were coming. With a common impulse the seated world rose to its feet. I heard a cleaving rush of sound, there was a lightning flash of brilliant hues,—then a vacancy, for a second, while the eye threw off its surprise and hurried to catch up with the flying cluster of meteors. They streamed away into the distance, closely pressed together; the colors became indistinguishable; they turned the half mile and disappeared for a few seconds behind an island of trees; then came in sight again beyond, and flew along past the belt of people banked together there; this belt instantly dissolved and flowed like a vast broken wave across the field to see the finish; the racers turned the corner, all in a close body and came booming down the home stretch under furious whip and spur, the riders leaning far forward and lashing with might and main; people began to ejaculate: "Red will win!" "Red's got it, sure!" A grand huzza was already rising for the red jacket, when all of a sudden, at the last possible moment, the orange rider threw in one supreme effort and shot by the red man like a thunderbolt. That stroke captured the $20,000, and the huzza already begun for red finished in a thunder-crash for orange.

Something followed, now, which was grand to see. The crowd overflowed into the race-course and packed it full—there was no longer a fence-line visible; people poured, in a thousand streams from over the field and everywhere and joined this throng; they even seemed to spring up out of the ground; the mass grew and grew, there below us, and became more and more compact, till at last it was like a solid black island of humanity in a level green sea of grass; it was said that there were 50,000 persons aggregated there; they stood closer together than the bristles in a brush, for they touched shoulders; their faces were all visible, for one half of the multitude were pressing to the left and the other to the right, all trying to reach the same point, the gateway under our stand—they wanted a good look at the winning horse. A narrow crack was left in this vast multitude, and through this the racers moved in a walk, in single file—it was as if the half hidden horses were swimming through it. A cheer rolled continuously along abreast the winner, and only ceased when he passed under the grand stand and disappeared. I came curiously near winning four pairs of gloves on this memorable race; twelve horses ran, and if they had dashed up to the winning-post from the opposite direction the horse I betted on would have been in the lead.

The island of humanity began to crumble away at the edges; it melted off in grains, driblets, cakes and blocks, and floated across the plain toward a wide, yellow, empty gap in the forest; little by little the scattered wreck thickened and compacted itself into a broad raft, more than half a mile long, one of whose extremities filled up and hid the yellow gap in the woods, while the other end was joined to the still steadily crumbling and still mighty mass in the field. The wide gap had been yellow, before, it was black, now—an almost motionless black stream, for the distance was so great that it had the still look of inert matter, unless one watched it sharply and intently a while—then one detected that it was dimly alive all over with minute writing movements, much as if it were a bed of worms. It was hard to believe, after watching that place for an hour, and detecting no change in it, that it was not stationary matter, but matter which had been changed and renewed every second, during all that time; it seemed odd and unbelievable that swiftly moving carriages should make so steadfast and motionless a spectacle.

At the end of an hour the mass was still crumbling, the debris was still stretching unbroken across the plain, and the gap was as full and black as ever. We descended, then, and joined the monster caravan.

Some of the "turn-outs" were peculiar. I saw a family of four or five persons wedged neck-deep in a two-wheeled square box, like bottles in a basket, and this ugly and ridiculous cart was drawn by a pony the size of the average Newfoundland dog. There was one long vehicle, with seats running fore and aft, omnibus fashion, which was evidently a fine and costly affair, and it was filled with a very aristocratic company of ladies and gentlemen, if appearances go for anything; the horses were six in number, large and fine and glossy, and they bore outriders who wore a sort of Italian brigand costume, with a deal of fiery red and yellow in the elaborate trimmings. There were hundreds of private liveries, of course, but they were very subdued in tone—simple brown, or blue, or black, with metal buttons; even a "bug" on the coachman's hat was rather a rarity. Central Park, on a field day, makes a much gaudier show, in the matter of liveries. I saw only one set of carriage servants with plush knee-breeches and powdered hair. Imagine all this sombre simplicity in a land where dukes and such still exist.

Imagine it in a city where great nobles used to parade down street with trains of satin-clad servants reaching into the hundreds only a century or so ago.

One species of scenery was very common in our great procession, but not tiresome to the eye on that account. This was the solitary female. She was painted and powdered, she was upholstered regardless of expense—sometimes modestly, but usually the other way. She had her coachman and footman on the box, and another lackey behind her; she lolled back among her cushions in an almost reclining attitude, with her exposed satin-slippered foot resting on a silken pillow, and a complacent simper on her inane face; and from top-knot to toe she was looking what she was,—the true French Goddess of Liberty, hallowed by a thousand years of the nation's respectful recognition. She was out in very numerous force indeed. The case could not well be otherwise, when one reflects that by the last census it appears that every Frenchman over 16 years old and under 116 has at least one wife to whom he has not been married. This occasions a good deal of what we call crime and the French call sociability.

When we passed under that noble monument the Arch of Triumph, our mighty caravan was an unbroken mass, clear down the broad avenue to the Place de la Concorde. It must have been a wonderful sight from the top of the Arch; that high perch was black with people. All down the avenue the wide side-walks and all the windows of the lofty lines of buildings were filled with the young and the old dressed in their Sunday best, to view the show.

THE DEVIL'S GATE

The curious names of towns and villages along the route woke many a memory that had nothing in the world to do with them. Among the rest the story of the Devil's Gate. The miners near one of those sublime gorges which former earthquakes have cloven in the Sierra Nevadas, named the place with their usual felicity in that line. They called it by a Spanish name signifying Devil's Gate. They never dreamed they were doing any harm. But a religious newspaper in San Francisco printed an editorial in which they were called to account—not in angry language, but in arguments and reasonings kindly put. They were admonished that it was not meet that men should honor the father of sin by naming after him the stupendous works of the Creator.

The miners called a meeting—nothing is done in California without calling a meeting about it. There must be a free, open, expression of opinion. In old times they always called a meeting, even when they were going to lynch a man who needed the most salutary and immediate hanging. The miners felt that they had innocently done a grave wrong in naming the gorge as they had. They wished to show the editor of the religious paper that they were not bad deliberately, and that in reality they were always ready to do as nearly right as they could and go to all reasonable lengths to earn the good opinion of worthy men. They discussed the matter in the meeting. They talked the subject over earnestly and feelingly, and then, by solemn and unanimous vote, they changed that name to— JEHOVAH'S GAP.

THE SNOW-SHOVELERS

A peaceful Sabbath morning in the elegant-residence end of a large New England town. Time, 8 a.m. A deep shroud of new-fallen snow covers everything. To the limit of sight down the white avenues, not a creature is stirring, no life is visible. There is no wind, not even a zephyr; the stillness is profound. Presently, in the distance a negro appears upon Mr. Morgan's long frontage, and another one appears at the same time on Mr. Newton's long frontage. They disturb the Sabbath hush with a couple of muffled scrapes of their snow-shovels. They look up and discover each other. For the next half hour they lean upon their shovels and converse at long range in powerful voices. Now and then they spit on their hands, but that is as far as their activities get.

ALECK. Hyo, Hank, is dat you?

HANK. Hellow, Ellick—dat you? Is you a shovelin' for Misto Morgan?

ALECK. Dat's it.

HANK. Who gwyne to shovel for old Misto Higginson?

ALECK. *I* dno. Tain't me, *dat's* sho'. Yah-yah-yah!

HANK. Me, too. Yah-yah-yah! Man got to git up mighty early in de mawnin' to git *me* to shovel by de *job*, mind *I* tell you.

ALECK. Dat's me—every time! Ef a man want his snow shoveled by de job, let him go git somebody else; I ain't gwyne rassle round rackin *my* bones outer jint on no *job*, now you hear *me*!

HANK. No, *sir*! When you wants *me* to shovel snow, s'I, you'll pay me by de *hour*, s'I; en it's thutty *cents*, too, s'I, en don't you *fogit* it! Yah-yah-yah!

ALECK. Dat's it, dat's it! Dem's my senterments, en I gwyne to stick to 'em tell I bust. By de *job*! De *ideear*! Hit make me tired, dat kind er talk do. Say, Hank, is you ben down to de meet'n, las' night?

HANK. No, I hain't ben to no meet'n; I ain't hear noth'n 'bout it. I uz to de nigger ball.

ALECK. No—wuz you? Why, I uz dah, too; I hain't seed you. Whah wuz you?

HANK. Oh, jist a sloshin aroun', same as usual, en havin' a time. I uz dah plum tell it bust up—goin' on daylight. What's de meet'n you talkin 'bout?

ALECK. Dey uz two. One wuz de Anerkis'.

HANK. Anerkis?

ALECK. Yes. En de yuther one uz de Socialis'.

HANK. What's dem—Anerkis en Socialis'?

ALECK. Why, hain't you hear 'bout 'em? Whah you ben?—'sleep? Why, Hank, dey's all de talk.

HANK. Is dat so? Huccum I ain't hear noth'n 'bout 'em? But dis is de fust time, I clah to goodness. What do dey do, Elleck?

ALECK. Why, dey—dey—well, dey talk.

HANK. Is *dat* all?

ALECK. All, says you. Why, what you *want* 'em to do, Hank?—it's politics.

HANK. Oh. I didn't unstan'. Dat's diffunt. Well, den, what's de politics?

ALECK. Hit's to have everybody git along 'dout work.

HANK. [*Turned to stone in the act of spitting on his hands.*] Git—along—widout—WORK? Why work is de nobles' thing in dis worl'—I never *hear* sich dam foolishness!

ALECK. Dat's jist what *I* say! De very words! You shet a man off fum workin', s'I, en what's de good er dat man? he ain't *no* good, s'I.

HANK. Right you is. Hit's de work dat make him healthy, hit's de work dat keep him soun'. Ef a man's too ornery to work en yearn his honest livin', let him go en lay down en die, dern him, dem's *my* senterments.

ALECK. Mine too,—wid de bark on. Why Hank, ef I didn't work for my livin' I'd feel dat low down dat I couldn't look nobody in de face. But de Anerkis he say—

HANK. Dat's it, dat's it—what *do* de Anerkis say, Elleck?

ALECK. He say dey's too much wealth stribited aroun' mongst de yuther folks, en he gwyneter *have* some of it; en he ain't gwyne work no mo', nuther.

HANK. Well, ef dat don't beat me! He gwyneter have some of it; how he gwyneter *git* it?

ALECK. Say he gwyneter *take* it.

HANK. Good lan'! *Foce?*

ALECK. Dat's what he say; gwyne take it by foce.

HANK. Socialis' want some too?

ALECK. Deed he do.

HANK. How *he* gwyne git it?

ALECK. 'Suasion.

HANK. How 'suasion?

ALECK. 'Leck all de Socialis' gang to Congress en pass laws en divide up all de lan' en truck mongst everybody so nobody ain't bleeged to work no mo'.

HANK. Looky here, Elleck, hit make me sick; clah to goodness hit make me sick. What *is* dis worl' a comin' to, when de mos' honorables' thing *in* it—which is work—is gitt'n disrespectable?

ALECK. Dat's de talk! When a man—when a hones' hard-workin' man—

[*Discussion interrupted by the employers, who appear suddenly and put in a word.*]

EMPLOYERS. If you two loafers can't find anything better to do than lean on your tools and yell all day and disturb everybody, shoulder your shovels and pack out of this!

PROFESSOR MAHAFFY
ON EQUALITY

THE EQUALITY OF MAN.
[PROF. MAHAFFY OF DUBLIN AT CHAUTAUQUA.]

In the preamble of your great declaration of rights appears, I believe, the statement that all men are equal in the sight of God. That statement was borrowed not from the scriptures, but from the speculations of the French revolutionists, whose opinion on the subject was to my mind of very small value. You are fond of talking of the equality of all men. The longer I read history, and the more I look around society the more I see profound inequalities in men. It is not true that every man is equal in the sight either of God or of men. What do you mean by God's having a chosen people if that people have not enormous advantage over their neighbors? Is each man as handsome as his neighbor? Is each man as strong? Is each man as long-lived? Has each man lived in as good a climate? The differences among men are really enormous, and when you go into this question of primitive civilization and compare the natives who have received light from above and those who have not, you will agree with me that of all false platitudes that were ever circulated among a sane people none is more false than the usual adage about the equality of man. I suppose this is an awful heresy, but, at least, as long as I am in this country, I am a free man; so you will allow me to make a clean breast of it.

When Prof. Mahaffy set out to instruct the world about Greece, he began in a rational way: that is, by first instructing himself in his subject. Why would it not have been a good idea to take at least an infant course in American political ideas before setting out to tell Americans what they are? His mountain has been brought to bed of no "heresy," awful or otherwise, in the above rather premature lying-in. He has misinterpreted a dogma of our Constitution—and ludicrously, if I may be so frank. No American believes that men are born physically equal; and it was not needed that a prophet should come from Dublin to explain, and argue out, and prove, with naive and quaint elaboration, the impossibility of a thing whose impossibility not even the American cats had yet questioned. If he had taken only a thousandth of the trouble to inform himself about us which he took to inform himself about the Greeks, he would have found that the American dogma, rightly translated, makes this assertion: that every man is of right born free—that is, without master or owner; and also, that every man is of right born his neighbor's political equal—that is, possessed of every legal right and privilege which his neighbor enjoys, and not debarred from aspiring to any dignity to which his neighbor may attain. When a man accepts this rendering of that gospel, it is the same as proclaiming that he believes that whoever is born and lives in a country where he is denied a privilege accorded his neighbor—even though his neighbor be a king— is not a freeman; that when he consents to wear the stigma described by the word "subject," he has merely consented to call himself a slave by a gentler epithet; and that where a king is, there is but one person in that nation who is not a slave. Professor Mahaffy was right when he observed that as long as he is in this country he is not a slave; and he might have added, without straining our ideas of the truth, that this is his first experience of the condition. For we gratefully believe, and do confidently claim, that this is now the only considerable country in the world where no slave exists. We get a good deal of instruction, first and last, from the strayed or stolen or mislaid European, and as a rule we have been able to get some sort of profit out of it, but this time we do seem to have got left on our base, as the Archbishop of Canterbury would say. If this present instructor is one of the "natives who have received light from above," what must be the condition of those other natives "who have not"? Of course Chautauqua means well, but it will think twice before she runs this risk again. She gets off by luck, this time. But some day when she isn't thinking she will import a teacher who knows his subject, and then it will cost her a thousand dollars.

MARK TWAIN

INTERVIEWING
THE INTERVIEWER

I found the editor of the New York *Sun* throned in his sanctum. He had his brimless cap on—his thinking cap, he terms it, and well he may, for many an exquisite fancy has it hatched out in its time. He was steeped in meditation. He was arranging in his mind a series of those articles for his next day's paper which have made the *Sun* famous in the land and a welcome visitor in every cultivated home circle upon the continent—interesting murders, with all the toothsome particulars; libels upon such men and women as have deserved the attention by being prominently blameless; aggravated cases of incest, with improving and elevating details; prize fights, elucidated with felicitously descriptive technicalities; elaborate histories of executions, assassinations and seductions; zealous defences of Reddy the Blacksmith and other persecuted patrons of the *Sun* who chance to stumble into misfortune. A high and noble thing it is to be the chief editor of a great metropolitan two-cent journal and mould the opinions of the washer-women and achieve the applause of the bone and sinew of the back streets and the cellars. And when that editor is gifted with that endowment which we term Genius, verily his position is almost godlike. I felt insignificant in the company of Charles A. Dana—and who wouldn't?

I said:

"Sir, I am a stranger to you, but being a journalist in a small way myself, I have presumed upon this fellowship to intrude upon you, and beg, at the fountain-head of American journalism, for a few little drops of that wisdom which has enabled you to confer splendor upon a profession which groped in darkness till your *Sun* flamed above its horizon."

"Be seated, sir, be seated. Ask what you will—I am always ready to instruct the ignorant and inexperienced."

"To come at once to the point, and not rob of their intellectual sustenance the suffering millions of our countrymen who hang upon your editorials, I desire to know the secret of your success—I desire to know what course one must pursue in order to make the name of his paper a household word at every fireside and a necessity unto all creatures whose idea of luxury soars to the equivalent of two cents."

"My son, unto none but you would I reveal the secret. You have paid me the homage which the envious multitude of so-called journalists deny me, and you shall be rewarded. Let the others suffer. Listen. The first great end and aim of journalism is to make a *sensation*. Never let your paper go to press without a sensation. If you have none, make one. Seize upon the prominent events of the day, and clamor about them with a maniacal fury that shall compel attention. Vilify everything that is unpopular—harry it, hunt it, abuse it, without rhyme or reason, so that you get a sensation out of it. Laud that which is popular—unless you feel sure that you can make it unpopular by attacking it. Hit every man that is down—never fail in this, for it is safe. Libel every man that can be ruined by it. Libel every prominent man who dare not soil his hands with touching you in return. But glorify all moneyed scum and give columns of worship unto the monuments they erect in honor of themselves, for moneyed men will not put up with abuse from small newspapers. If an uncalled-for onslaught upon a neighboring editor who has made you play second fiddle in journalism can take the bread out of his mouth and send him in disgrace from his post, let him have it! Do not mind a little lying, a liberal garbling of his telegrams, a mean prying into his private affairs and a pitiful and treacherous exposure of his private letters. It takes a very small nature to get down to this, but I managed it, and you can—and it makes a princely sensation. If two prominent preachers solemnize a questionable deathbed marriage when custom does not require them to cipher at the rights of the case until it is too late and one of the parties dies, go for them! Make fiends of them! Howl, and gnash your teeth, and rave with virtuous indignation till you convince yourself that in spite of your native rottenness you have some of the raw material of a saint in you, after all. But if those preachers *refuse* to solemnize the marriage, and go driveling around after information till the bridegroom dies and the bride goes crazy, *then* you can howl with forty-fold power about the soulless inhumanity of those divines. Simply a little change of base and you can make it appear that nothing is so damnable as the spectacle of a preacher refusing a deathbed request of any kind for any reason whatsoever."

[Enter a Reporter.]

"Mr. D., there is a report that Gen. Grant was drunk yesterday."

"Is there any truth in it?"

"No, sir."

"Then publish it by all means—say it *is* true—make a sensation of it—invent affidavits."

[Exit Reporter.]

"Yes, my son, in journalism, the idea is to deal in injurious personalities as much as you can, but you must make it a point to pitch into the helpless—it is the safest course. Make yourself a sort of Ishmael; have no friendships that are worthy; praise nothing that is worthy of praise; hate everything that other men love; cackle your opinions upon all subjects and upon all occasions with a swaggering pretense that the people attach weight to them; delve among forbidden subjects and revel among their filth, for it is the life of a two-cent paper; uncover all rapes and seductions, and expose them to the public gaze. In a word, be shameless—have this virtue and you need no other to make a two-cent paper succeed. And as soon as success is achieved, the illustrated papers will print your picture and publish your startlingly eventless biography, written by yourself."

[Enter a Reporter.]

"Mr. D., Gen. W. is dead."

"Ah, that is fortunate. A dangerous man—a very danger-ous man. But now we can settle with him. Write an abusive obituary, and traduce the character of his mother."

"And Mr. Greeley has fallen on the ice and hurt himself seriously."

"Ah, that is fortunate also. State that he was under the in-fluence of liquor. I wish we could do something to make the *Tribune* notice us."

[Exit Reporter.]

"Another feature, my son, is the interviewing business. We used to do a good thing in that line, but latterly *Sun* reporters find it difficult to get access to respectable people. However, it matters little. We seldom printed what people actually said, anyhow, and so we can get up the interviews just as well in the office as elsewhere. Try your hand at it—I think you will like it. Journalism, my son, is a great business—a very great business—and I feel that I do not flatter myself when I say that I have made of the New York *Sun* an entirely unique pa-per—nothing like it ever existed before, out of perdition. It is a wonderful newspaper. And I could have made just such a one out of that Chicago *Republican* if they had let me stay, but that story they got up there about my having an improper intimacy with the aged chief of police angered me to such a degree that I would not remain. The whole city regretted my departure, and so did the newspaper men. The papers published kindly and appreciative farewells, and some of them were very touching. One paper published a long and flattering biography of me, and said in conclusion: 'We deeply regret the departure of this gifted writer from our midst. We have seen meaner men than him—we have seen much meaner men than Charles A. Dana—though we cannot recall an instance just now.' For the first time in many years I shed tears when I read that article."

[Enter a Reporter.]

"Mr. D., Mark Twain is dead—at least it is so reported."

"Is that so? Well, we have nothing against him—he never did any good. Publish an apparently friendly obituary of him—and say at the end that we are pained to have to state that for many years he gained his livelihood by the nefarious practice of robbing graveyards. That will be sufficient—I have already dished *him* up in a column editorial about his imbecile article upon the 'Cuban Patriot.'"

I said: "Mr. D., I beg pardon for mentioning it, but *I* am that Mark Twain to whose remains you propose to give a unique and pleasant interest, and I am not dead."

"Oh, you are the person, are you?—and you are not dead?

Well, I am sorry, but I cannot help the matter. The obituary must be published. We are not responsible for your eccentricities. You *could* have been dead if you had chosen—nobody hindered you. The obituary is fair game, for whatever is Rumor to another paper is Fact to the *Sun*. And now that you are here handy, I will interview you. Please to give me the details of any aggravated or unnatural crimes you may have committed."

AN INCIDENT

Sunday morning, Sept. 11, 1887, in Elmira, N.Y., I got the largest and gratefulest compliment that was ever paid me. I walked down to State street at 9.30, with the idea of getting shaved. I was strolling along in the middle of Church street, musing, dreaming; I was in a silent Sabbath solitude. Just as I turned into State, I looked up and saw a mighty fire-boy ten or twelve steps in front of me, creeping warily in my direction, with intent eye, and fingering the lock of a gun which was concealed behind him, all but the end of the barrel, which stuck up into view back of his shoulder. My instant thought was, "he is a lunatic out gunning for men, and I cannot escape." He stopped, bent his body a little, and brought his gun to the front, cocked. There was no time to consider impulses; I acted upon the first one that offered. I walked straight to him, with a beating heart, and asked him to let me look at his weapon. To my joy, he handed it to me without a word. I turned it about, this way and that, praising, examining, asking question after question, to keep his attention diverted from murderous ideas until somebody should come by. He answered right along, and soon I caught a blessed sound: I understood him to say he was out hunting cats. He added, "There they are, yonder;" and turned and pointed. I saw four sorry-looking cats crossing the street in procession some forty steps away. I forgot my own troubles for a moment, to venture a plea for the cats; but before I could get it out, he interrupted with the remark that those were our "engine-house cats," and went on to say that they were not afraid of dogs or any other creature, and followed him around every morning while he shot their breakfast—English sparrows. He called, "Come, Dick!" and Dick came, and so did the rest. Aha!—so far from being a madman, he was saner, you see, than the average of our race; for he had a warm spot in him for cats. When a man loves cats, I am his friend and comrade, without further introduction. So I dropped the barber-shop scheme, and Hercules and I went promenading up and down the Sunday stillnesses, talking, and watching for sparrows, while the four cats followed in patient procession behind. I made so many intelligent observations about cats, that I grew in the estimation of Hercules, right along—that was plain to see; but at last in an unlucky moment I dimmed and spoiled this effect by letting out the fact that I was a poor shot and had no improvable talent in that line. I saw in a flash the damage I had done myself, and hastened to switch off onto something else and try to get back my lost ground. I praised the gun again, and asked where I could get one like it. The address given was unfamiliar to me, but I said,—

"I can manage it, though; for Mr. Langdon or Mr. Crane will know."

Hercules came to a sudden stop; ordered arms; leaned on his gun, and began to inspect me with a face all kindled with interest. He said:

"Do you live up on the East Hill with Mr. Crane, summers?"

"Yes."

"No! But is—is it *you?"*

I said yes, and he broke all out into welcoming smiles, and put out his hand and said heartily:

"Well, here I've been poking round and round with you and never once— Look here, when a man's done what *you've* done, he don't need to give a *damn* whether he can shoot or not!"

What an immense compliment it was!—that "Is it *you?*" No need to mention names—there aren't two of you in the world! It was as if he had said, "In my heedlessness I took you for a child's toy-balloon drifting past my face—and Great Scott, it's the moon!"

A consciously exaggerated compliment is an offence; but no amount of exaggeration can hurt a compliment if the payer of it doesn't know he is exaggerating. In fact, if he can superbly *seem* unconscious, he may depend upon it that even that will answer. There is the instance of that minister of Napoleon's who arrived late at the council board at a time when six kings were idling around Paris waiting for a chance to solicit concessions and relaxings of one sort or another. The emperor's brow darkened and he delivered a thunder-blast at the procrastinating minister; who replied with apparently unstudied simplicity—

"Sire, at any other court I had not been late. I hurried as I could, but my way was obstructed by the concourse of tributary kings!"

The brow of the master of the world unclouded. *I* know how good he felt.

THE JUNGLE
DISCUSSES MAN

It was in the jungle. The fox had returned from his travels, and this great assemblage had gathered from the mountains and the plains to hear the wonders he was going to tell about the strange countries he had seen and the wide oceans he had crossed. As he walked slowly up and down the grassy space reserved for him, turning his subject over in his mind and arranging his thoughts, he was the centre and focus of an absorbing interest. All eyes followed him back and forth, and the light of admiration was in them, and in some a frank glint of envy. It was not to be denied that contact with the great world had had a gracious and elevating effect upon him. His carriage was graceful, mincing, polished and elegant beyond anything that had been seen in the back woods before; his manners were dignified, easy, and full of distinction; his speech was flowing and unembarrassed, and his foreign accent, so far from marring it, added a delicate charm to it.

It was a fine audience. In front, in the place of honor, was the king, the elephant; to his right and left, all around the front row, sat the nobility, the great beasts of prey; back of these, row after row, disposed according to rank and order of precedence, were the other creatures. In front of the king stood the royal chaplain, the marabout, on one leg, and with his eyes closed in meditation. After a time Reynard opened his portfolios and got out his collection of pictures, and was now ready to begin. The marabout asked a blessing, then the king said to Reynard—

"Begin!"

The first picture represented a soldier with a gun, a missionary following him with a book. It was passed around, and all examined it with interest.

"What are these things?" the king inquired. "Creatures?"

"Yes, your majesty."

"What kind? How are they called?"

"Sometimes men, sometimes Christians. It is all the same."

"What are they made of?"

"Flesh and bones, like your majesty's subjects."

The tiger reached for the picture and examined it again, with a new interest.

"They look good, these Christians," he said, licking his lips; "are they good?"

"Better than any other of God's creatures, my lord. It is their constant boast; it is a cold day when they forget to give themselves that praise."

The tiger licked his lips again, exhibiting much excitement, and said—

"I would God I had one."

The lion said—

"It is my thought, brother."

The gorilla, leaning upon his staff, examined the picture thoughtfully, his great lips retiring from his tushes and exposing a fellowship smile which some of the smaller animals tremble at and wish they were at home.

"They go upright—like me," he said. "Is it so?"

"They do, my lord."

"Is it feathers they are covered with—or fur?" inquired the rhinoceros.

"Neither, your grace. It is an artificial material, called

clothing. They make it themselves, out of various stuffs, and they can take it off when they want to; their natural covering is fish-skin."

Everybody was astonished, and said—

"It doesn't belong to them!" "They can take it off!" "They don't have to put it on, and yet they do!" And the gorilla said, impressively, "Well, I'll be damned!"

The marabout lifted his skinny lids and gave him a crushing look, and he apologised. A hairless dog remarked—

"One perceives that they live in a cold country; that is why they put it on."

"No," observed Reynard; "they put it on in the hottest countries, just the same."

"Why, that is silly!" said many voices. "Why do they afflict themselves in that way?"

"Because they are ashamed to be seen naked."

There was a blank look on all the faces. They could not understand this. Then they all began to laugh, and several said—

"Since they can take those things off when they want to, don't they sometimes want to, and don't they do it?"

"Yes, often—in privacy."

There was another great laugh, and many said—

"Don't they know that God sees them naked?"

"Certainly."

"Land! and they don't mind *Him*? It must be a dirty-minded animal that will be nasty in God's presence and ashamed to be nasty in the presence of his own kind."

I RISE TO A QUESTION
OF PRIVILEGE

EDS. NEWS LETTER: Is it not possible that your journal, which is usually more mathematically accurate in its statements than even I am, has made a mistake for once? A paragraph in your last issue suggests this. I append it:

> TWAIN will kindly remark that a communication, signed as a communication, does not admit the editorial We. Whereby, a portion of his esteemed favor is unavailable.

I do not remember sending you a communication. I have been too busy of late to write communications to anyone but the person a curl from whose chignon I wear next my heart.

Someone has been trying to write himself rich over my sig-
nature, and I am glad that his foolish idea that because Twain
means two it was good grammar for him to call himself We,
wrought his downfall and brought failure upon his impos-
ture. I would not have mentioned this matter but for the fact
that I am just now smarting under a thing which makes me
particularly bitter against all forms of misstatement whatsoever. Friends of mine are attributing to me a remark which I
solemnly protest I never made. It was made by a comrade of
mine in the Holy Land. If you will permit me, I will tell the
circumstances precisely as they occurred, and thus free myself
from any blame in the matter, if there *is* really anything to be
blamed for in it. One of my comrades, "Jack," was a boy of
eighteen, and just as good a boy as ever was. He was an innocent cub, and was always floundering into mistakes that
brought him trouble. He was always dropping absurd and ill-
timed remarks without ever meaning any harm, and so he was
always being scolded and harried and lectured by the pilgrims
in the party. They liked him, and knew he meant well, and
they did this for his own good, and never in an unkind spirit.
In their fervent apostrophes to noted localities, the pilgrims
often let fall startling statements that Jack had never heard
before, or else had forgotten, and therefore, they surprised

him into saying many things whose absurdity he could see when it was too late. Jack always listened attentively, and with a desire to learn. This is the circumstance:

One day when we were camped at Jericho, near the Jordan, a pilgrim said: "Those mountains yonder on the opposite side of the valley, are the Mountains of Moab, where Moses lies secretly buried."

"Moses who?"

"Jack, if you were not so astonishingly innocent, I would rebuke you for asking such a question. Moses was the great leader of the children of Israel."

"Oh, I know, now—I recollect. He was a good man—they called him the Meek. Well, what did he do?"

"He led the children of Israel up out of the wilderness."

"That was good. Go on, please."

"On the other side of those mountains, Jack, is a desert. It is three hundred miles across it from here to the land of Egypt. The children of Israel entered Canaan at this place where we are when they came out of that desert. That great chief, Moses, staid with them, all through that weary march of forty years, and his wisdom, more than any other human aid, guided them safely and wonderfully to the Promised Land. It was a great task, but splendidly did Moses perform it."

"What, forty years? Only three hundred miles? Why, Ben Holladay would have fetched them through in thirty-six hours!"

We did not laugh, because Jack was very sensitive about his blunders. He was merely given to understand that he must not make damaging comparisons between Moses and Ben Holladay, and there the matter dropped. But here, all of a sudden, this anecdote, all garbled and mutilated, turns up in San Francisco, and *I* am accused of making that remark. I did *not* make it, and never thought of making it. I get enough abuse, without having to suffer for the acts of others. I acknowledge that I have written irreverently, but I did it heedlessly, or when out of temper—never in cold blood. I *did* fail somewhat in reverence for Jacob, whose character all the bookmakers praise so highly, but that was honest. I revered the *really* holy places, and deliberately and intentionally derided only the manifest shams. The bookmakers all deride them in private conversation, themselves, but weep over them in their books. I am acquainted with some of those people, and I speak by the card. A missionary in Constantinople, a personal friend of the Rev. Mr. Prime, told me that that favorite Palestine authority used to read his lugubrious chapters aloud, after he had written them, and then laugh at the fine humor of flooding them with tears which came wholly from his inkstand. Any unprejudiced person who reads his *Tent Life in the Holy Land* will not doubt that statement. That sentimental fire-plug would have gone entirely dry if he had actually shed half the tears there are in his book. Deceived by that book, our passengers really felt that they were lacking in depth of feeling because they could not cry. They went about trying to cry, they sincerely wanted to cry, they often hoped, and promised and threatened to cry, but they always failed to connect. They were members of the church, and had a genuine reverence for sacred things, but they found at last, that it is possible for sound veneration to exist below the water level.

If the Rev. Dr. Thomas, who gave me such a terrific setting-up in his sermon last Sunday night—and in very good grammar, too, for a minister of the gospel—had only traveled with me in the Holy Land, I could have shown him how much real harm is done to religion by the wholesale veneration lavished upon things that are mere excrescences upon it; which mar it; and which should be torn from it by reasoning or carved from it by ridicule. They provoke the sinner to scoff, when he ought to be considering the things about him that are really holy. It is all very well to respect the devotee's feelings, but let us have a thought for the sinner's failings, in the meantime—he has a soul to be saved, as well as the devotee. Remove the things that seduce his attention from objects that are truly holy. Increase his chances for salvation, even though the means resorted to to do it may cause the devotee a pang. The devotee being safe, had better in charity suffer a little, than that the sinner be damned. The devotee learns his unreasoning, uncriticising veneration in unthinking infancy; and that he possesses it, is no merit of his; but the matured sinner can only learn to reverence such things as his thinking and reasoning faculties teach him are worthy of it. If I could, I would make such havoc among the shams of Palestine that I would leave little there for men to feast their eyes and feed their fancies upon save the Hill of Calvary, and the lesson it carries to the most careless heart that pulses in its presence. I would leave it to tell of Him who suffered there, and to suggest the picture of the Crucifixion more vividly than the multitude of its surroundings, which are at best of questionable holiness, can ever do. All things must pass away but that one Figure, and when they do, the world will be none the loser for it.

The day shall come when the families of Shechem, whose genealogical trees were hoary with age when Christ talked with their ancestor at the well of Samaria, shall have passed from earth and been forgotten; when the Oaks of Mamre shall mark no more the grave of Jacob, and the tomb of his Rebekah shall arrest no curious wayfarer from Bethlehem to the City of David; when the awful march of Joshua from the Waters of Merom to Baal-Gad shall be a vague tradition, and the shepherds of Anti-Lebanon no longer see his shadowy armies sweep by in the mists of the night; when Jerusalem shall have crumbled to dust and the place of the Manger passed from the knowledge of men; when the history of all Israel shall be as the secret sepulchre the Mountains of Moab hide in their solitudes—yet still, serenely above the waste and ruin of the ages, the Teacher of Nazareth, standing upon the height of Calvary—sacred because the theatre of the noblest self-sacrifice man has yet conceived—shall say to them that mourn this desolation, "Peace! *I* am the Resurrection and the Life!"

In that day, reverence will be offered where it of right belongs.

But excuse me. I have wandered a little from my subject. It is sound parliamentary human nature, though. There was never a legislator yet who could rise to a question of privilege and stick to the matter of it.

MARK TWAIN

TELEGRAPH DOG

It was in the time of the Indian war, a quarter of a century ago. Company C, 7th Cavalry, 45 strong, had been
headed off by a body of well armed Indians numbering 600
seasoned warriors, and had taken sanctuary in a small island
in the South Platte a hundred miles from the nearest army
post. Their situation was critical, and from day to day it grew
worse; for their supply of provisions was slender, and a couple
of attempts to get word to the fort had failed. This during the
first twelve days. The Indians appeared in force every morning
at a judicious distance beyond the river in the plain, and for
hours kept up a long-range rifle practice upon the camp. The
sharp-shooters of Company C wasted no ammunition—it
was too scarce and too precious for that; they only fired when

they were nearly sure of their man; the intervals between their shots were wide, but the shots were deadly. In the course of a day's work they bagged many Indians, while the reckless storm of Indian bullets harvested but a small crop of casualties by comparison. Yet the general result was against the soldiers, for to them the loss of a man was a serious matter, whereas to the enemy the loss of a dozen was of no considerable consequence.

Sometimes the Indians, driven to fury by the stubborn resistance of the handful of whites cast their native caution aside for a moment and dashed through the shallow stream and tried to storm the camp—but in broad day always; so the whites were ready for them, and flung them back defeated, each time.

At the end of three weeks the soldiers were in sorry case. Their commander was lying in the protection of a pit hollowed in the sand, helpless, with both legs broken by balls; eight of his men were dead, twelve were wounded, five of them to disablement; of the twenty-nine still ranking as effectives one was departing under cover of the night to try and carry word to the fort, and the rest were weak from insufficient nourishment and from want of due rest and sleep; the horses were all dead and were serving as breast works and food.

Now came a lull. The plains were silent, the enemy had vanished. This continued all day. In some breasts it raised a hope—perhaps the Indians had seen smoke-signals warning them of the approach of white reinforcements and had given up and taken themselves off. It was a fair surmise, but some of the old hands said it could mean something of a different sort. Jack Burdick said—

"They can be hatching something outside of their own usages. There's a couple of white renegades with them."

The remark made an impression.

"It's so," said several: "we can't prophesy what Indians will do when they've that kind of cattle on hand to help invent projects."

There was silence for a while and much reflection. Then Phil Cassidy began—

"If Captain Johnson would let one of us slip over there to-night and—"

"Well, he won't," said Jack Burdick with decision, "so you can drop that notion."

It was dropped, and there was another silence. A hundred yards away, down among a growth of young cottonwoods the barking of a dog broke out of the stillness, in a series of strange, sharp, broken notes.

"At it again," said Tom Hackett.

"Yes," said another; "time-keeper of the camp; when he begins, you know it's sundown."

"Practicing his voice—been an opera dog, Sandy says; expects to get an engagement again when the war's over."

"Not in the way of singing, I reckon," said Hackett; "it's too jerky and broken-up; the most undoglike racket I've ever heard out of a dog's mouth."

"Sandy calls it staccato—says that's its scientific name."

"It's a bright little chap, anyway; Sandy talks to him the same as if he was a human."

"Yes, and what's more, he understands—understands every word. He can say to him, 'Now Billy, you go and snoop around in the bushes at the head of the island, and if you don't smell Injuns over on the shore, speak up and say so;' and the dog will trot right off, and by and by you'll hear him bark, sure enough, showing that he got the whole idea and is furnishing the facts."

A doubter laughed, and said—

"You idiot, *that* don't prove anything. How'd you know whether he was telling the truth or not."

The rest laughed, and the witness "schwieg," as the Germans say, and seemed sorry he had said anything.

"Say—the sun's down and he's at it yet. . . . . . There, he's stopped, but it's too late. Poor little doggy. It's an awful pity."

"By George, it just is! Why, hang it, we *can't* get along without the little cuss—he's just a dear, and the friendliest little thing—"

"Just the life of the camp. Right you are, Jack Burdick. Blamed if I couldn't 'most cry."

"What in the nation has possessed Sandy, to let the poor little fellow break the orders?"

"Oh, you can bet on it he ain't with him, or he wouldn't."

"Well, maybe the captain—just this once—"

"No—you needn't imagine it," said Jack Burdick sorrowfully, "he loves the little dog, and it'll hurt him in his heart, but that don't matter; duty is duty, discipline is discipline, and if his own brother broke an order he'd have to take the proceeds."

The men sighed, and said—

"It's so. Poor little chap! He *was* so friendly and sociable."

"And is so brave, too. On hand in every scrimmage, like a little man, and fetching things for Sandy, and just as active and satisfied as if it was play."

"Yes, and didn't give a dern for bullets, poor little rat—let them whiz all around him and just 'tended to business, and helped the best he could," said Jake Foster, in an unsteady voice, for he was only a youth.

Meantime, down in the cottonwood growth Sandy was saying to the dog—

"Now you've got your instructions, Billy. Do everything the way I told you. The camp's life is in your hands—in your paws, you understand. Keep me posted, that's a good dog. They're coming! Kiss me good-bye, and away you go!"

Footsteps came grinding through the sand, and a soldier said—

"I'm to kill him, Sandy—it's the captain's orders. I wish it was somebody else."

"Too late, 'Rastus, he's gone."

"Gone where?"

"Gone over to the Indians. Deserted."

"Deserted? Him? Billy? It's a lie; he wouldn't. Sandy, you *made* him."

"Well, it's true. I did. It was to save him. He disobeyed orders."

"I reckon you'll be sent for, corporal—just as well come along now."

Which he did; and reported to the captain, who said—

"I am disabled, and in pain—make quick talk—explain this matter."

The corporal's explanation was not over-clear, and contained traces of lying. The captain degraded him to the ranks, and ordered him on outpost duty; and added, sharply—

"If I have to use a spy, I'll risk *your* person in place of a better man."

"Let me try it to-night, sir."

"What?"

"To-night, sir."

"Do you mean it?"

"Yes, sir."

"Why, this is—is handsome. I'd give anything to know—to know what this tranquillity means. Come—try it, man, try it! But look sharp, don't get yourself caught; we can't spare a man."

The men soon knew of the dog's escape and were glad; and of the corporal's reduction, and were sorry.

. . .

Three hours later, Billy's distant bark was heard from beyond the river, and it rejoiced the hearts of the men to know he was alive and out of reach of the executioner. His clack went on during a stretch of fifteen minutes; then Sandy emerged from an ambush among the undergrowth on the head of the island and went groping his way in the dark to the captain's pit, answering the challenges of the sentinels as he came. His report was important:

"The renegades have persuaded them to a night attack, sir."

"Oh, impossible!"

"I heard the renegades talking it over, sir, and it will begin at two in the morning."

"Do you mean that you have been—"

"I have been in their camp, sir." This was not true. "It is in a deep swale in the plain, two miles up to the right, beyond where the big cottonwoods are, in the bend."

"You have done admirably, I must say—and bravely."

"They are coming in their full strength, sir; half will cross the river at the ford half a mile up, and slip down behind us; and at the signal they are going to spring their surprise in the dark, front and rear."

"It is hardly believable—for Indians—but no matter, we'll prepare."

Half of the effectives took position on one side of the island, under lieutenant Burr, the other half on the other side under lieutenant Taylor; a man crossed the river, on each side, and stole out in the gloom and crouched in the grass—no more than these could be spared for picket duty. The two repelling detachments lay on their arms and waited in profound silence.

Toward two o'clock the pickets stole in and reported the advance of the Indians. After what seemed a long interval, and was a trying and tedious one to the watchers, a multitude of dim forms appeared upon either bank, and crept noiselessly down to the water, and came gliding across like spirits. Nearer and nearer they approached the prone watchers; nearer and still nearer, until the front rank of each mass was within thirty feet of their fate; then Burr gave the signal, two sheets of fire glared out upon the night from the repeating rifles, and glare followed glare, crash followed crash, and the Indians fell by winrows.

The survivors broke away whooping and yelling and disappeared in the darkness. The camp was saved. The ex-corporal was reinstated in his rank.

.   .   .

No Indians came the next day. They were busy at home, wailing for their dead. The renegades were busy, too. They were smoothing down the anger of the chiefs and trying to explain the miscarriage of their scheme.

"There is a traitor in the camp," they said.

"Then find him," said the unpleasant chiefs, with rude brevity, "or pay with your scalps."

They found the man they believed to be the right one. He

suffered death, and the chiefs were satisfied. With the traitor out of the way, another surprise could be ventured with safety, and it was decided upon.

At night fall Sandy asked Captain Johnson's leave to go spying again, and got it with grateful promptness. He went to his lair at the head of the island and waited. About ten o'clock his dog's distant note came down to him on the faint wind, from over the plain, and presently he rose and crept back to camp and reported to the captain.

"I have been in their midst, sir," he said, with economy of truth, "and have heard them talk. They are wild with rage over their disaster. The renegades have told them we know Indians too well to believe they will try another night surprise—at least any time *soon;* that we shall be all asleep to-night, and not dreaming of attack; therefore to-night, of all nights, is the time to try again. The chiefs are persuaded, sir, and game is called for one o'clock."

His words were true, and at the named hour there was another double slaughter of savages and a complete victory. When the matter was finished, Captain Johnson sent for Sandy. There the wounded officer lay in his pit, worn and haggard and pale, but there was almost the vigor of health in his voice when he said—

"I have sent for you to thank you. The medicine chest is by

me here, if you can see it—it will answer for a seat. Sit down, sir."

"In your presence, sir?"

"Certainly, sir. I have promoted you. You are a captain, now."

．　．　．

The next day the whites had another ominously quiet day, but not so the Indians. Their rage was such that they were almost beyond control. Dark looks were cast upon the renegades, and for a time, near the close of the day, their lives were in danger; but they had a grisly repute as necromancers, and they invoked the evil spirits with awful and spectacular ceremonies and got information which saved them. The spirits said there was still another traitor in the camp, and pointed him out—he was a dead man in five minutes; and they devised a trick upon the whites, and commanded its execution. The chiefs listened to its sombre details, found them to their taste, and promised humble obedience.

About this time or a little later, Captain McGregor, by permission of Captain Johnson, was starting out spying again. He hid himself in his usual lair, and at ten Billy's crackling bark began once more to rise upon his listening ear out of the murky remotenesses of the prairie. By and by it ceased, and

Captain McGregor betook himself to Captain Johnson's pit, sat down on the medicine case, and reported.

"I have just come from their camp, sir, and they have contrived a fresh trick. They will try it, and they are our meat, to a certainty. At noon tomorrow all the six chiefs and thirty-five picked braves will come disguised as decrepit old squaws, under a truce-flag, and beg for leave to wail for their dead and bury them. They will have knives, tomahawks and revolvers under their ragged robes. They will offer to place half of their number in our hands on the island, to remain while the rest wail and do the burying. When the hostages have reached the island they will pull their weapons and begin the rush, and the others will raise the war-whoop and follow."

"It ends the campaign; triumph is sure, and the merit is yours, sir. Tomorrow I shall know how to reward you to your full deserving if all goes as we now expect. For the present I will limit myself to thanking you for to-day's high service, *Colonel* McGregor."

. . .

Toward ten, next morning, the glasses showed a slow-moving and apparently bent and rickety body of ancient squaws approaching across the plain. They were expected, and their intended request would be granted. They plodded on. Some distance to their right the two renegades walked slowly along watching them, and talking, the dog Billy at their heels. One of them presently said—

"Suppose they fail?"

"But they won't; there aren't any spies to give it away this time, that is sure."

"Still, I say it again: suppose they fail?"

"Well, what then?"

"Shall you want to see the inside of that Injun camp again?"

"Well—no. No, it wouldn't do. We shouldn't pull through alive this time, I reckon. What do you suggest?"

"I don't quite know. How would this do? Stop where we are, and wait till they do the rush. It'll all be over in five minutes. If we hear the victory-song, go and join them and help do the shouting. If we don't hear it, make for the lower ford and break for a safe country."

"That'll answer. I'm agreed."

They stopped. The dog trotted on ahead and sat down on a knoll a hundred yards away. One of the men said—

"There is that strange dog that is always around under our heels and has that broken-up bark."

"Yes, and only barks at night. I'm superstitious about him, George; we've had worse and worse luck from the time he came."

"It's so, Peter. I never thought of it before. I wish we had killed him."

"It's not too late, yet."

"Come, then."

"Wait a minute—he's trotting off. Let him settle again."

The dog disappeared beyond the hillock. The men waited a long time, scanning the region everywhere, but there was no dog to be seen. Then Peter said—

"Well, it serves us right. We had our chance and didn't use it. He is a devil in disguise, probably, and won't give us another; for I can tell you one thing about that kind of evil spirits, they—"

A distant crash of guns broke the sentence in two. Then another and another; then an unpunctuated confusion of popping shots and war-whoops which continued during several minutes, then died down, and silence ensued. The two men waited, breathless, for the victory-song. In place of it rose the white man's hurrah.

"It's all up!" said Peter. "Come—no time to waste!"

"Wait—there's that dog-bark again."

"Come along! If—"

"Wait, I tell you—I've got the secret. I've been a telegraph operator; *he's barking the Morse system.*"

"Bosh! Come—we *must* be moving!"

"Listen! 'G-u-a-r-d l-o-w-e-r f-o-r-d—r-e-n-e-g-a-d-e-s—' What did I tell you? He has blocked the lower ford against us. We must make for the upper one. Come along."

They started on a run.

"Hi—yonder's the dog!"

"In range, too—let him have it!"

Billy was running. The third shot brought him down with a broken leg. They were soon out of sight, and safe to make the ford if not interrupted. Billy tried to correct his recent telegram, but his pains broke up his message and he had to give it up.

In the white camp all was joy and gladness; victory was with the flag, and the perilous campaign was over. Captain Johnson called all the survivors before him, and in their presence conferred upon Colonel McGregor the rank of Major General in the Regular Army.

The Tenth Cavalry arrived before night, and the happiness of the brave little band was complete.

Toward noon the next day the little dog appeared upon the bank of the stream and lay down there, exhausted with pain and the slow labor of dragging himself so far. He was afraid to go nearer the camp anyway until he should get a pardon, for he knew that he was under sentence of death, and that military customs are strict. He hoped for a pardon, though, and expected it, and was soldier enough to wait patiently.

Major General McGregor sent for him and would have pardoned him; but when he saw that his leg was broken it seemed best to shoot him; which he did, and Billy died licking his hand and looking his love for him out of his fading eyes.

THE AMERICAN PRESS

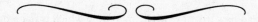

Goethe says somewhere that "the thrill of awe"—that is to
say, REVERENCE—"is the best thing humanity has."
—MATTHEW ARNOLD.

I should say that if one were searching for the best means to
efface and kill in a whole nation the discipline of respect, one
could not do better than take the American newspapers.
—MATTHEW ARNOLD.

RESPONSE.

Mr. Arnold judged of our newspapers without stopping to
consider what their mission was. He judged them from the
European standpoint; and he could not have found an impro-
perer one to judge an American newspaper from.

Take the most important function of a journal in any country, and what is it? To furnish the news? No—that is secondary. Its first function is the guiding and moulding of public opinion, the propagating of national feeling, and pride in the national name—in a word, the keeping the people in love with their country and its institutions, and shielded from the allurements of alien and inimical systems. If this premiss be granted—and certainly none will deny it—Mr. Arnold mistook for a flaw in our journalism a thing which is not a flaw at all, but its supremest merit.

In Constantinople there was a newspaper some years ago—a kind of a newspaper—and it may be there yet, though the climate was pretty rugged for it. That little paper could shout as vigorously as it wanted to when it was praising our Holy Established Church of Mahomet; or lauding the sublimities of the Sultan's character and virtues; or describing how the nation adored the dust he walked upon; or what grief and dismay swept the land when he was ill for a couple of days; and it could branch out and tell tales and invent stories— pious, guileful, goody-goody nursery tales showing how odious and awful are all forms of human liberty, and how holy and healthy and beautiful is the only right government, the only true and beneficent government for human beings— a despotism; a despotism invented by God, conferred directly by the grace of God, nourished, watched over, by God; and to criticise which, is to utter blasphemy. It was working its function, you see—keeping the people's ideas in the right shape. But there were things which it might not shout about—things concerning which it must be judiciously blind, and deaf, and most respectfully quiet. Now would you look for a joke, or lightsome chaff, or a frivolous remark, in that journalistic hearse? You would be disappointed; it was not the place for it. An Arctic gravity, decorum, reverence, was its appointed gait: for the devil's aversion to holy water is a light matter compared with a despot's dread of a newspaper that laughs. Does this description describe the Turkish journal? It does. Does it describe the Russian journal? It does. Does it describe the German journal? It does. Does it describe the English journal? With unimportant modifications, it does. If the flies in a spider's web had a journal, would it describe that one, too? It would. By the language of that journal you would get the idea that to a fly's mind—a fly in a web—there is nothing in the world that is quite so winsome, and gracious, and provocative of gushing and affectionate reverence, as a great gilt-backed, steel-fanged, well-intrenched spider.

The chief function of an English journal is that of all other journals the world over: it must keep the public eye fixed admiringly upon certain things, and keep it diligently diverted from certain others. For instance, it must keep the public eye fixed admiringly upon the glories of England, a processional splendor stretching its receding line down the hazy vistas of time, with the mellowed lights of a thousand years glinting from its banners; and it must keep it diligently diverted from the fact that all these glories were for the enrichment and aggrandizement of the petted and privileged few, at cost of the blood and sweat and poverty of the unconsidered masses who achieved them but might not enter in and partake of them. It must keep the public eye fixed in loving and awful reverence upon the throne, as a sacred thing, and diligently divert it from the fact that no throne was ever set up by the unhampered vote of a majority of any nation, and that hence no throne exists that has a right to exist, and no symbol of it, flying from any flagstaff, is righteously entitled to wear any device but the skull and cross-bones of that kindred industry which differs from royalty only business-wise—merely as retail differs from wholesale. It must keep the citizen's eye fixed in reverent docility upon that curious invention of machine politics, an Established Church, and upon that bald contradiction of common justice, a hereditary nobility; and diligently divert it from the fact that the one damns him if he doesn't wear its collar, and robs him under the gentle name of taxation whether he wears it or not, and the other gets all the honors while he does all the work.

Dear me, the dignity, the austerity, the petrified solemnity which Mr. Arnold admired and estimated as a merit in the English press, is not a merit, it is inseparable from the situation. Necessarily, journalism under a monarchy can do its hard duty and perform its grotesque function with but one mien—a graveyard gravity of countenance: to laugh would expose the whole humbug. For the very existence of a sham depends upon this cast-iron law—that it shall not be laughed at. And its prosperity depends upon this other law—that men shall speak of it with bated breath, respectfully, reverently: according to the gospel of Matthew Arnold and Goethe the poet.

Mr. Arnold, with his trained eye and intelligent observation, ought to have perceived that the very quality which he so regretfully missed from our press—respectfulness, reverence—is exactly the thing which would make our press useless to us if it had it—rob it of the very thing which differentiates it from all other journalism on the globe and makes it distinctively and preciously American. Its frank and cheerful irreverence is by all odds the most valuable quality it possesses. For its mission—overlooked by Mr. Arnold—is to stand guard over a nation's liberties, not its humbugs and shams. And so it must be armed with ridicule, not reverence. If during fifty years you could impose the blight of English journalistic solemnity and timid respect for stately shams upon our press, it is within the possibilities that the republic would perish; and if during fifty years you could expose the stately and moss-grown shams of Europe to the fire of a flouting and scoffing press like ours, it is almost a moral certainty that monarchy and its attendant crimes would disappear from Christendom.

Well, the charge is, that our press has but little of that old-world quality, reverence. Let us be candidly grateful that this is so. With its limited reverence it at least reveres the things which this nation reveres, as a rule, and that is sufficient: what other people revere is fairly and properly matter of light importance to us. Our press does not reverence kings, it does not reverence so-called nobilities, it does not reverence established ecclesiastical slaveries, it does not reverence laws which rob a younger son to fatten an elder one, it does not reverence any fraud or sham or infamy, howsoever old or rotten or holy, which sets one citizen above his neighbor by accident of birth; it does not reverence any law or custom, howsoever old or decayed or sacred, which shuts against the best man in the land the best place in the land and the divine right to prove property and go up and occupy it. In the sense of the poet

Goethe—that meek idolater of provincial three-carat royalty and nobility—our press is certainly bankrupt in the "thrill of awe"—otherwise reverence: reverence for nickle-plate and brummagem. Let us sincerely hope that this fact will remain a fact forever: for to my mind a discriminating irreverence is the creator and protector of human liberty—even as the other thing is the creator, nurse, and steadfast protector of all forms of human slavery, bodily and mental.

I believe it is our irreverent press which has laughed away, one by one, what remained of our inherited minor shams and delusions and serfages after the Revolution, and made us the only really free people that has yet existed in the earth; and I believe we shall remain free, utterly free and unassailably free, until some alien critic with sugared speech shall persuade our journalism to forsake its scoffing ways and serve itself up on the innocuous European plan. Our press has done a worthy work; is doing a worthy work; and so, though one should prove to me—a thing easily within the possibilities—that its faults are abundant and over-abundant, I should still say, no matter: so long as it still possesses that supreme virtue in journalism, an active and discriminating irreverence, it will be entitled to hold itself the most valuable press, the most wholesome press, and the most puissant force for the nurture and protection of human freedom that either hemisphere has yet produced since the printer's art set itself the tedious and disheartening task of righting the wrongs of men.

To gather into a sheaf the random argument which I have left scattered behind me over the field: I take issue with the old-world doctrine of Goethe and Mr. Arnold, that reverence has but one office—to elevate. It has more than one. There is a reverence which elevates, there is a reverence which degrades. To pay reverence to a man who has done sublime work for his race and his generation, even though he were born as poor and nameless as that plodding German who invented the movable types, and so by his single might lifted a flaming intellectual sun into a zenith where mental midnight had reigned before, elevates him who pays it; but to pay reverence to a mere king, or prince, or duke, or any other empty accident, must degrade and does degrade any man or nation that pays it. And I am not able to believe that any intelligent man has ever lived within this superstition-dissipating century—even Goethe—who paid it and was not secretly ashamed of it.

THE CHRISTENING YARN

The brief anecdote with a smart surprise at the end of it is common. Common and good; but it is not nearly so good nor so well worth the teller's best art and the listener's best attention as is the *long* anecdote with a smart surprise at the end. Examples of this breed are scarce—in fact very scarce. I call to mind only three, and two of the three fail oftener than they win. This is natural, for when a story is long and elaborate, a sharp listener has a chance to put this and that together as you go along and guess-out your surprise before you get to it yourself. I will not waste space on the two doubtful examples; let us take up No. 3, the infallible. Its structure is such that it is a sure card; it will catch the listener every time; there is no way for him to cipher out what the surprise is going to be. I got this one from Mr. Bram Stoker when he first came over with Mr. Irving years ago. There are two ways of telling it—the quiet way and the violent way. The former is Mr. Stoker's way and the latter is mine. Mr. Stoker's way requires an exact memory, for his version has humorous points scattered all through it, and of course a point that is not delivered in its own proper language is no point at all and works damage. I have a bad memory and cannot memorize things; but as this story is a speech, and as I am purposely careful to make not a single point anywhere except at the tail-end, no memory is required—a new speech every time will answer every purpose.

The story is about a christening. The scene is a humble house in a village. The place is crowded with the family's friends and neighbors. The little minister takes the baby from the father's hands and holds it out on his palms and contemplates it some little time in silence, his inspiration-mill pumping away, meantime, and getting him ready for the greatest effort of his life. He is a spread-eagle orator with a good opinion of his powers, and he proposes to make the most of this opportunity. Now then, pupil of mine, I desire you to get up and hold out the imaginary baby on your palms and make this minister's speech. I wish you to begin impressively, and speak slowly; warm up gradually; become fiery, impetuous; get carried clear out of yourself by your own eloquence—and so, storm along, all the way down to the climax. I wish you to be apparently absolutely serious; put in no shade or suggestion of humor anywhere. I wish you to string the speech out until you see by the faces of the audience that all expectancy of fun has faded out of their minds, and that they have come to the conclusion that no fun was intended; that you are making the speech for its own sake and are proud of it, thinking it to be noble and stirring eloquence. Within a few moments you will see another fact steal into their intent faces: the fact that they are disappointed in you; that they pity you and are ashamed of you. This is what you are after—your prey is secure, now—it is the victorious moment: strike! Cut the speech short where you are and spring the climax. You'll see what will happen:

THE CHRISTENING.

Ah, my friends, he is but a little fellow. A very little fellow. Yes—a v-e-r-y little fellow. *But!* [With a severe glance around.] What of that! I ask you, What of *that!* [From this point, gradually begin to rise—and soar—and be pathetic, and impassioned, and all that.] Is it a crime to be little? Is it a *crime*, that you cast upon him these cold looks of disparagement? Oh, reflect, my friends—reflect! Oh, if you but had the eye of poesy, which is the eye of prophecy, you would fling your gaze afar down the stately march of his possible future, and *then* what might ye not see! *What?* ye disparage him because he is *little?* Oh, consider the mighty ocean! ye may spread upon its shoreless bosom the white-winged fleets of all the nations, and lo they are but as a flock of insects lost in the awful vacancies of interstellar space! Yet the mightiest ocean is made of *little* things; *drops*—tiny little drops—each no bigger than the tear that rests upon the cheek of this poor child! And oh, my friends, consider the mountain ranges, the giant ribs that girdle the great globe and hold its frame together—and what are they? Compacted grains of sand—*little* grains of sand, each no more than a freight for a gnat! And oh, consider the constellations!—the flashing suns, countless for multitude, that swim the stupendous deeps of space, glorifying the midnight skies with their golden splendors—what are *they?* Compacted motes! specks! impalpable atoms of wandering star-dust arrested in their vagrant flight and welded into solid worlds! *Little* things; yes, they are made of *little* things. And he—oh, look at him! *Little,* is he?—and ye would disparage him for it! Oh, I beseech you, cast the eye of poesy, which is the eye of prophecy, into his future! Why, he may become a poet!—the grandest the world has ever seen—Homer, Shakspeare, Dante, compacted into one!—and send down the procession of the ages songs that shall contest immortality with human speech itself! Or, he may become a great soldier!—the most illustrious in the annals of his race—Napoleon, Caesar, Alexander compacted into one!—and carry the victorious banner of his country from sea to sea, and from land to land, until it shall float at last unvexed over the final stronghold of a conquered world!—oh, heir of imperishable renown! Or, he may become a—a—he—he—[struggle desperately, here, to think of something else that he may become, but without success—the audience getting more and more distressed and worried about you all the time]—he may become—he— [suddenly] *but what is his name?*

Papa [with impatience and exasperation]. His *name*, is it? Well, his name's *Mary Ann!*

MARK TWAIN

THE WALT WHITMAN CONTROVERSY

SIR: I have seen, thus far, only one remotely reasonable argument in justification of the law's letting old obscene books alone and tomahawking new ones. It is this: the old ones merely (and innocently) mirrored the life of their times, and the indecencies in them were not written with the intent to defile the reader's mind. Hence they were harmless. That is the one apparently reasonable argument which I have thus far encountered. But when you come to examine it carefully, it seems to be quite insufficient. For this reason: we surely do not make laws against the *intent* of obscene writings, but against their probable *effect*. If this is true, it seems to follow that we ought to condemn all indecent literature, regardless of its date. Because a book was harmless a hundred years ago, it does not follow that it is harmless to-day. A century or so ago, the foulest writings could not soil the English mind, because it was already defiled past defilement; but those same writings find a very different clientage to work upon now. Those books are not dead; among us they are bought and sold and read, every day.

If you will allow that the question of real importance is, Which are more harmful, the old bad books or the new bad books? permit me, then, to note some particulars, and institute some comparisons.

I begin with a glance among my book shelves, and at the end of five minutes I have selected and laid out the following volumes—and without a doubt I could have found them in your library in less time:

Tom Jones.

Joseph Andrews.

Smollett's Works.

Shakspeare.

Byron.

Burns.

Gulliver's Travels.

Walpole's Letters.

Mémoires de Casanova.

De Foe's Moll Flanders.

Balzac's Droll Tales.

Rabelais.

The Heptameron.

The Decameron.

Arabian Nights.

Les Cent Nouvelles Nouvelles.

The Satyricon of Petronius Arbiter.

Of course I could find a good deal more of this sort of literature in my library and yours, but this batch is sufficient for my purpose.

Next, I turned my attention to new bad books. At the moment, I was able to call only three to mind—Swinburne's and Oscar Wilde's Poems, and Walt Whitman's "Leaves of Grass." Did I lay out these with the others? No—for I didn't have them. Have you? Are they handy for the average young man or Miss to get at? Perhaps not. Are those others? Yes, many of them.

Now I think I can show, by a few extracts, that in the matters of coarseness, obscenity, and power to excite salacious passion, Walt Whitman's book is refined and colorless and impotent, contrasted with that other and more widely read batch of literature.

In "Leaves of Grass," the following passage has horrified Mr. Oliver Stevens by its coarseness:

* * * * * * * * * * * *

* * * * * * * * * * * *

[We are obliged to omit it.—ED. POST.]

It does seem unnecessarily broad, it is true; but observe how pale and delicate it is when you put it alongside this passage from Rabelais—thirteenth chapter. (Hotten's London edition is illustrated by Doré, and the pictures have carried it all over the world):

" 'How is that?' said Grangousier. 'I have,' answered Gargantua, 'by a long and curious experience, found out a means to—' "

* * * * * * * * * * * *

* * * * * * * * * * * *

[We think it best to omit the rest of it.—ED. POST.]

Or this, from Gulliver's Travels, (chapter V, Brobdignag,) a book which is in everybody's house and is daily read by old and young alike:

"Neither did they [the naked young maids of honor,] at all scruple, while I was by,—"

* * * * * * * * * * * *

* * * * * * * * * * * *

[We cannot venture to complete the above extract.
—ED. POST.]

Now what do you really think of those?—especially the one from the popular Doré Rabelais. Yet you know that that isn't the nastiest thing in American libraries, by any means. No, for there is a story told in the Heptameron, and retold in several other books, which easily surpasses it in filthiness. Under the title of "Merrie Jests of King Louis the Eleventh," it appears in Balzac's "Droll Tales," (illustrated by Doré,) and may be found and consulted in almost anybody's house—for the Droll Tales are in the shelves of a multitude of elegant people who wouldn't dare to be caught sheltering a copy of Leaves of Grass in these fastidious days.

But enough of obscenity; you perceive, yourself, that Whitman knows nothing about the genuine article. Let us now consider erotic matters. Whitman's offenses in this line are contained in the following passages:

* * * * * * * * * * * *

* * * * * * * * * * * *

[All things considered, it seems best to omit them.
—ED. POST.]

In our households, one young person in a hundred and fifty thousand has the opportunity to read those passages;

but every creature in every household in America has the opportunity to read the following lines from Shakspeare (Venus and Adonis),—and it won't stir him up, either, because it was not written with the *intent* to stir people up:

"The boar!" quoth she; whereat a sudden pale,

* * * * * * * * * * * * *

Usurps her cheeks; she trembles at his tale,
And on his neck—

* * * * * * * * * * * * *

* * * * * * * * * * * * *

[This is not proper matter for the columns of the EVE-NING POST, and we must be excused from printing the remainder of the passage.—ED. POST.]

Is that healthy poetry for the young? Is there an educated young fellow of nineteen, in the United States, who has not read Venus and Adonis? I pray you let us not deceive ourselves: he does not exist. You diligently hunted out all the improprieties in Shakspeare and the Bible before you were nineteen—you remember it well, now that I call your attention to it—and do you believe that you and I were any more opulently stocked with the naturalest kind of human nature than is this new generation? Go to; the thought is foolishness.

Now, let us plunge into the Heptameron—at random—it is all alike. Try this, from Tale XLVI:

"Going up a little wooden staircase, he found—"

* * * * * * * * * * * * *

* * * * * * * * * * * * *

[It is too strong; we cannot print it.—ED. POST.]

After that, Whitman is delicate enough, isn't he? Now try this, (The Venial Sin,) from Balzac's Droll Tales—illustrated by Doré, and to be found everywhere:

"This time the said youth * * *, and even ventured so far as to verify if—"

* * * * * * * * * * * * *

* * * * * * * * * * * * *

[But that is even stronger; we cannot consent to complete the quotation.—ED. POST.]

How does "The Venial Sin" strike you? Does anything in Leaves of Grass approach it for evil effectiveness? And while you have the Droll Tales in your hand, please glance at the second picture on page 211. And read the story, too, by way of conviction. Boccaccio is in everybody's library, and is praised by Macaulay and other great authorities. I have an English copy, but have mislaid it; so if you will allow me, I will make an extract from a French copy which was lent me by a neighboring clergyman some time ago. It is a story about a verdant young girl and a young hermit. Try this passage:

"L'hermite se déshabille aussitôt, et le petit ange d'en faire autant. Quand ils sont tout nus l'un et l'autre, Rustique se met à genoux, et fait placer la pauvre innocente vis-à-vis de lui, dans la même situation. Là les mains jointes, il promène ses regards sur—"

* * * * * * * * * * * * *

* * * * * * * * * * * * *

[It is impossible to print the rest—we must be excused.—ED. POST.]

It is rather a long story, but I thought I would put it all in, just to show that when it comes to doing the erotic, Walt Whitman's ink is altogether too pale. Now let us finish by dipping just once into that richest of all rich mines—I mean, of this kind of literature—Casanova's Memoires. From chapter V:

"Ravi d'avoir savouré * * * * * * que je venais de goûter complètement pour la première fois, je—"

* * * * * * * * * * * * *

* * * * * * * * * * * * *

[This is too horrible; let it stop there; we cannot finish the story. We are sorry we cannot better assist our correspondent to make out his argument, but indeed his citations, admirable as they are for the purpose in view, are altogether too strong for a newspaper like ours.—ED. POST.]

There—I have finished my quotations. And now I suspect that you will not dare to print them in full. As likely as not, you will cut them down to next to nothing, or even leave them out altogether. But if you do, I shall not complain; for such a course will formidably fortify my position, since it will show that you know, quite well, that antiquity and absence of evil intent can't take the harmfulness out of indelicate literature. Yes, you know that indecent literature is indecent literature; and that the effects produced by it are exactly the same, whether the writing was done yesterday or a thousand centuries ago; and that these effects are the same, whether the writer's intent was evil or innocent.

Whitman's noble work

DISCUSSION GUIDE

1. In both "An Incident" (1887) and "Frank Fuller and My First New York Lecture" (1895), Twain discusses notions of his own fame. How did his perception of his fame change from one essay to the next? Do you get the impression that Twain wants to be a celebrity?

2. What does "Conversations with Satan" tell us about Twain's ideas of consumerism? What is the point of the story about the cigars? How does it relate to his initial discussion with Satan about German heaters?

3. In "The Privilege of the Grave," Twain writes, "Free speech is the privilege of the dead, the monopoly of

the dead. They can speak their honest minds without offending" (page 58). What is Twain saying about the right to free speech in America? Do you agree with him? Why or why not?

4.   In "The Quarrel in the Strong-Box," Twain writes, "This fable teaches us that the character of the Equality established by our laws is commonly misunderstood on both sides of the water; and not oftener by the ignorant than by the ostensibly wise" (page 76). What does this statement mean? What point is he making with this essay?

5.   The essay "Dr. Van Dyke as a Man and as a Fisherman" retells an argument between Twain and Henry van Dyke, a Presbyterian clergyman, in which the two men discuss their different views of mankind. With whom did you side in the argument? Why?

6.   What do we learn about Twain's religious beliefs from the two essays "The Missionary in World-Politics" and "Dr. Van Dyke as a Man and as a Fisherman"? Explain what Twain means when he writes at the end of "The Missionary in World-Politics": "The time is grave. The future is blacker than has been any future which any person now living has tried to peer into" (page 109).

7. What is the moral of the story "The Undertaker's Tale"? Who is the "pleasant new acquaintance" (page 111) who tells the story?

8. In "Professor Mahaffy on Equality," Twain argues against Mahaffy's take on the American notion of freedom. Who do you agree with? Are all men in America born free? In what different ways could someone be considered "not free" without being a slave?

9. The essay "Interviewing the Interviewer" takes on the sensational media of Twain's day. Has the media changed since the essay was written in 1870? Which of Twain's arguments is still relevant today? Which is not?

10. Why do you think this collection of Twain's writing was titled *Who Is Mark Twain*? What do we learn about the author from these writings?

11. Many of Twain's essays express his views about issues of the media, religion, and politics of his time. Do you feel that his commentaries apply to modern-day issues? Which of his essays feel like they could have been written in the twenty-first century?

ABOUT MARK TWAIN

SAMUEL LANGHORNE CLEMENS was born on November 30, 1835, in the village of Florida, Missouri. He attended the ordinary western common school until he was twelve, the last of his formal schooling. He became a typesetter and began work on his brother's Hannibal newspaper, publishing his first humorous sketch in 1851. In the next fifteen years, he was successively a steamboat pilot, a soldier for three weeks, a silver miner, a newspaper reporter, and a bohemian in San Francisco known as "Mark Twain." At no time during these years did he seriously entertain a career in literature. But in 1865, deeply in debt, he acknowledged a talent for "literature, of a low order—i.e. humorous." In the next forty years, he published more than a dozen books and hundreds of shorter works, including his masterpiece in 1885, *Adventures of Huckleberry Finn*. Seven years before Clemens died in 1910, Rudyard Kipling told an American publisher: "He is the biggest man you have on your side of the water by a damn sight, and don't you forget it."